NIGHTMARE ABBEY

THOMAS LOVE PEACOCK

WILDSIDE PRESS

Doylestown, Pennsylvania

Nightmare Abbey was first published in 1818, and lightly revised in 1837 by the author.

There's a dark lantern of the spirit,
Which none see by but those who bear it,
That makes them in the dark see visions
And hag themselves with apparitions,
Find racks for their own minds, and vaunt
Of their own misery and want.

— BUTLER

MATTHEW. Oh! it's your only fine humor, sir. Your true melancholy breeds your perfect fine wit, sir. I am melancholy myself, divers times, sir; and then do I no more but take pen and paper presently, and overflow you half a score or a dozen of sonnets at a sitting.

STEPHEN. Truly, sir, and I love such things out of measure.

MATTHEW. Why, I pray you, sir, make use of my study; it's at your service.

STEPHEN. I thank you, sir, I shall be bold, I warrant you. Have you a stool there, to be melancholy upon?

— BEN JONSON,
Every Man in his Humor,
Act 3, Sc. 1

Chapter I

Ay esleu gazouiller et siffler oye, comme dit le commun proverbe, entre les cygnes, plutoust que d'estre entre tant de gentils po'tes et faconds orateurs mut du tout estime.

— Rabelais, *Prol.* L. 5

Nightmare Abbey, a venerable family mansion, in a highly picturesque state of semi-dilapidation, pleasantly situated on a strip of dry land between the sea and the fens, at the verge of the county of Lincoln, had the honor to be the seat of Christopher Glowry, Esquire. This gentleman was naturally of an atrabilarious temperament, and much troubled with those phantoms of indigestion which are commonly called "blue devils." He had been deceived in an early friendship: he had been crossed in love; and had offered his hand, from pique, to a lady, who accepted it from interest, and who, in so doing, violently tore asunder the bonds of a tried and youthful attachment. Her vanity was gratified by being the mistress of a very extensive, if not very lively, establishment; but all the springs of her sympathies were frozen. Riches she possessed, but that which enriches them, the participation of affection, was wanting. All that they could purchase for her became indifferent to her, because that which they could not purchase, and which was more valuable than themselves, she had, for their sake, thrown away. She discovered, when it was too late, that she had mistaken the means for the end — that riches, rightly used, are instruments of happiness, but are not in themselves happiness. In this willful blight of her affections, she found them valueless as means: they had been the end to which she had immolated all her affections, and were now the only end that remained to her. She did not confess this to herself as a principle of action, but it operated through the medium of unconscious self-deception, and terminated in inveterate avarice. She laid on external things the blame of her mind's internal disorder, and thus became by degrees an accomplished scold. She often went her daily rounds through a series of deserted apartments, every creature in the house vanishing at the creak of her shoe, much more at the sound of her voice, to which the nature of things affords no simile; for, as far as the voice of woman, when attuned by gentleness and love, transcends all other sounds in harmony, so far does it surpass all others in discord, when stretched into unnatural shrillness by anger and impatience.

Mr. Glowry used to say that his house was no better than a spacious kennel, for every one in it led the life of a dog. Disappointed both in love and in friendship, and looking upon human learning as vanity, he had come to a conclusion that there was but one good thing in the world, videlicet, a good dinner; and this his parsimonious lady seldom suffered him to enjoy: but, one morning, like Sir Leoline in *Christabel,* 'he woke and found his lady dead,' and remained a very consolate widower, with one small child.

This only son and heir Mr. Glowry had christened

Scythrop, from the name of a maternal ancestor, who had hanged himself one rainy day in a fit of *tædium vitæ*, and had been eulogized by a coroner's jury in the comprehensive phrase of *felo de se*; on which account, Mr. Glowry held his memory in high honor, and made a punchbowl of his skull.

When Scythrop grew up, he was sent, as usual, to a public school, where a little learning was painfully beaten into him, and from thence to the university, where it was carefully taken out of him; and he was sent home like a well-threshed ear of corn, with nothing in his head: having finished his education to the high satisfaction of the master and fellows of his college, who had, in testimony of their approbation, presented him with a silver fish-slice, on which his name figured at the head of a laudatory inscription in some semi-barbarous dialect of Anglo-Saxonized Latin.

His fellow students, however, who drove tandem and random in great perfection, and were connoisseurs in good inns, had taught him to drink deep ere he departed. He had passed much of his time with these choice spirits, and had seen the rays of the midnight lamp tremble on many a lengthening file of empty bottles. He passed his vacations sometimes at Nightmare Abbey, sometimes in London, at the house of his uncle, Mr. Hilary, a very cheerful and elastic gentleman, who had married the sister of the melancholy Mr. Glowry. The company that frequented his house was the gayest of the gay. Scythrop danced with the ladies and drank with the gentlemen, and was pronounced by both a very accomplished charming fellow, and an honor to the university.

At the house of Mr. Hilary, Scythrop first saw the beautiful Miss Emily Girouette. He fell in love; which is nothing new. He was favorably received; which is nothing strange. Mr. Glowry and Mr. Girouette had a meeting on the occasion, and quarreled about the terms of the bargain; which is neither new nor strange. The lovers were torn asunder, weeping and vowing everlasting constancy; and, in three weeks after this tragical event, the lady was led a smiling bride to the altar, by the Honorable Mr. Lackwit; which is neither strange nor new.

Scythrop received this intelligence at Nightmare Abbey, and was half distracted on the occasion. It was his first disappointment, and preyed deeply on his sensitive spirit. His father, to comfort him, read him a Commentary on Ecclesiastes, which he had himself composed, and which demonstrated incontrovertibly that all is vanity. He insisted particularly on the text, "One man among a thousand have I found, but a woman amongst all those have I not found."

"How could he expect it," said Scythrop, "when the whole thousand were locked up in his seraglio? His experience is no precedent for a free state of society like that in which we live."

"Locked up or at large," said Mr. Glowry, "the result is the same: their minds are always locked up, and vanity and interest keep the key. I speak feelingly, Scythrop."

"I am sorry for it, sir," said Scythrop. "But how is it that their minds are locked up? The fault is in their artificial education, which studiously models them into mere musical dolls, to be set out for sale in the great toy-shop of society."

"To be sure," said Mr. Glowry, "their education is not so well finished as yours has been; and your idea of a musical doll is good. I bought one myself, but it was confoundedly out of tune; but, whatever be the cause, Scythrop, the effect is certainly this, that one is pretty nearly as good as another, as far as any judgment can be formed of them before marriage. It is only after marriage that they show their true qualities, as I know by bitter experience. Marriage is, therefore, a lottery, and the less choice and selection a man bestows on his ticket the better; for, if he has incurred considerable pains and expense to obtain a lucky number, and his lucky number proves a blank, he experiences not a simple, but a complicated disappointment; the loss of labor and money being superadded to the disappointment of drawing a blank, which, constituting simply and entirely the grievance of him who has chosen his ticket at random, is, from its simplicity, the more endurable." This very excellent reasoning was thrown away upon Scythrop, who retired to his tower as dismal and disconsolate as before.

The tower which Scythrop inhabited stood at the southeastern angle of the Abbey; and, on the southern side, the foot of the tower opened on a terrace, which was called the garden, though nothing grew on it but ivy, and a few amphibious weeds. The southwestern tower, which was ruinous and full of owls, might, with equal propriety, have been called the aviary. This terrace or garden, or terrace-garden, or garden-terrace (the reader may name it ad libitum), took in an oblique view of the open sea, and fronted a long tract of level seacoast, and a fine monotony of fens and windmills.

The reader will judge, from what we have said, that this building was a sort of castellated abbey; and it will probably, occur to him to inquire if it had been one of the strongholds of the ancient church militant. Whether this was the case, or how far it had been indebted to the taste of Mr. Glowry's ancestors for any transmutations from its original state, are, unfortunately, circumstances not within the pale of our knowledge.

The northwestern tower contained the apartments of Mr. Glowry. The moat at its base, and the fens beyond, comprised the whole of his prospect. This moat surrounded the Abbey, and was in immediate contact with the walls on every side but the south.

The northeastern tower was appropriated to the domestics, whom Mr. Glowry always chose by one of two criterions, — a long face, or a dismal name. His butler was Raven; his steward was Crow; his valet was Skellet. Mr. Glowry maintained that the valet was of French extraction, and that his name was Squelette. His grooms were Mattock and Graves. On one occasion, being in want of a footman, he received a letter from a person signing himself Diggory Deathshead, and lost no time in securing this acquisition; but on Diggory's arrival, Mr. Glowry was horror-struck by the sight of a round ruddy face, and a pair of laughing eyes. Deathshead was always grinning, — not a ghastly smile, but the grin of a comic mask; and disturbed the echoes of the hall with so much unhallowed laughter, that Mr. Glowry gave him his discharge. Diggory, however, had staid long enough to make conquests of all the old gentleman's maids, and left him a flourishing colony of young Deathsheads to join chorus with the owls, that had before been the exclusive choristers of Nightmare Abbey.

The main body of the building was divided into rooms of state, spacious apartments for feasting, and numerous bedrooms for visitors, who, however, were few and far between.

Family interests compelled Mr. Glowry to receive occasional visits from Mr. and Mrs. Hilary, who paid them from the same motive; and, as the lively gentleman on these occasions found few conductors for his exuberant gaiety, he became like a double-charged electric jar, which often exploded in some burst of outrageous merriment to the signal discomposure of Mr. Glowry's nerves.

Another occasional visitor, much more to Mr. Glowry's taste, was Mr. Flosky,* a very lachrymose and morbid gentleman, of some note in the literary world, but in his own estimation of much more merit than name. The part of his character which recommended him to Mr. Glowry, was his very fine sense of the grim and the tearful. No one could relate a dismal story with so many minutiæ of supererogatory wretchedness. No one could call up a raw-head and bloody-bones with so many adjuncts and circumstances of ghastliness. Mystery was his mental element. He lived in the midst of that visionary world in which nothing is but what is not. He dreamed with his eyes open, and saw ghosts dancing round him at noontide. He had been in his youth an enthusiast for liberty, and had hailed the dawn of the French Revolution as the promise of a day that was to banish war and slavery, and every form of vice and misery, from the face of the earth. Because all this was not done, he deduced that nothing was done; and from this deduction, according to his system of logic, he drew a conclusion that worse than nothing was done; that the overthrow of the feudal fortresses of tyranny and superstition was the greatest calamity that had ever befallen mankind; and that their only hope now was to rake the rubbish together, and rebuild it without any of those loopholes by which the light had originally crept in. To qualify himself for a coadjutor in this laudable task, he plunged into the central opacity of Kantian metaphysics, and lay perdu several years in transcendental darkness, till the common daylight of common sense became intolerable to his eyes. He called the sun an ignis fatuus; and exhorted all who would listen to his friendly voice, which were about as many as called "God save King Richard," to shelter

---

* A corruption of Filosky, quasi *Philoskios,* a lover, or sectator, of shadows.

themselves from its delusive radiance in the obscure haunt of Old Philosophy. This word Old had great charms for him. The good old times were always on his lips; meaning the days when polemic theology was in its prime, and rival prelates beat the drum ecclesiastic with Herculean vigor, till the one wound up his series of syllogisms with the very orthodox conclusion of roasting the other.

But the dearest friend of Mr. Glowry, and his most welcome guest, was *Mr. Toobad,* the Manichæan Millenarian. The twelfth verse of the twelfth chapter of Revelations was always in his mouth: "Woe to the inhabiters of the earth and of the sea! for the devil is come among you, having great wrath, because he knoweth that he hath but a short time." He maintained that the supreme dominion of the world was, for wise purposes, given over for a while to the Evil Principle; and that this precise period of time, commonly called the enlightened age, was the point of his plenitude of power. He used to add that by and by he would be cast down, and a high and happy order of things succeed; but he never omitted the saving clause, "Not in our time"; which last words were always echoed in doleful response by the sympathetic Mr. Glowry.

Another and very frequent visitor, was the Reverend Mr. Larynx, the vicar of Claydyke, a village about ten miles distant; — a good natured accommodating divine, who was always most obligingly ready to take a dinner and a bed at the house of any country gentleman in distress for a companion. Nothing came amiss to him, — a game at billiards, at chess, at draughts, at backgammon, at piquet, or at all fours in a tête-à-tête, — or any game on the cards, round, square, or triangular, in a party of any number exceeding two. He would even dance among friends, rather than that a lady, even if she were on the wrong side of thirty, should sit still for want of a partner. For a ride, a walk, or a sail, in the morning, — a song after dinner, a ghost story after supper, — a bottle of port with the squire, or a cup of green tea with his lady, — for all or any of these, or for any thing else that was agreeable to any one else, consistently with the dye of his coat, the Reverend Mr. Larynx was at all times equally ready. When at Nightmare Abbey, he would condole with Mr. Glowry, — drink Madeira with Scythrop, — crack jokes with Mr. Hilary, — hand Mrs. Hilary to the piano, take charge of her fan and gloves, and turn over her music with surprising dexterity, — quote Revelations with Mr. Toobad, — and lament the good old times of feudal darkness with the transcendental Mr. Flosky.

Chapter II

Shortly after the disastrous termination of Scythrop's passion for Miss Emily Girouette, Mr. Glowry found himself, much against his will, involved in a lawsuit, which compelled him to dance attendance on the High Court of Chancery. Scythrop was left alone at Nightmare Abbey. He was a burnt child, and dreaded the fire of female eyes. He wandered about the ample pile, or along the garden-terrace, with "his cogitative faculties immersed in cogibundity of cogitation." The terrace terminated at the southwestern tower, which, as we have said, was ruinous and full of owls. Here would Scythrop take his evening seat, on a fallen fragment of mossy stone, with his back resting against the ruined wall, — a thick canopy of ivy, with an owl in it, over his head, — and the Sorrows of Werter in his hand. He had some taste for romance reading before he went to the university, where, we must confess, in justice to his college, he was cured of the love of reading in all its shapes; and the cure would have been radical, if disappointment in love, and total solitude, had not conspired to bring on a relapse. He began to devour romances and German tragedies, and, by the recommendation of Mr. Flosky, to pore over ponderous tomes of transcendental philosophy, which reconciled him to the labor of studying them by their mystical jargon and necromantic imagery. In the congenial solitude of Nightmare Abbey, the distempered ideas of metaphysical romance and romantic metaphysics had ample time and space to germinate into a fertile crop of chimæras, which rapidly shot up into vigorous and abundant vegetation.

He now became troubled with the passion for reforming the world.* He built many castles in the air, and peopled them with secret tribunals, and bands of illuminati, who were always the imaginary instruments of his projected regeneration of the human species. As he intended to institute a perfect republic, he invested himself with absolute sovereignty over these mystical dispensers of liberty. He slept with Horrid Mysteries under his pillow, and dreamed of venerable eleutherarchs and ghastly confederates holding midnight conventions in subterranean caves. He passed whole mornings in his study, immersed in gloomy reverie, stalking about the room in his nightcap, which he pulled over his eyes like a cowl, and folding his striped calico dressing gown about him like the mantle of a conspirator.

"Action," thus he soliloquized, "is the result of opinion, and to new-model opinion would be to new-model society. Knowledge is power; it is in the hands of a few, who employ it to mislead the many, for their own selfish purposes of aggrandizement and appropriation. What if it were in the hands of a few who should employ it to lead the many? What if it were universal, and the multitude were enlightened? No. The many must be always in leading-strings; but let them have wise and honest conductors. A few to think, and many

---

* See Forsyth's *Principles of Moral Science.*

to act; that is the only basis of perfect society. So thought the ancient philosophers: they had their esoterical and exoterical doctrines. So thinks the sublime Kant, who delivers his oracles in language which none but the initiated can comprehend. Such were the views of those secret associations of illuminati, which were the terror of superstition and tyranny, and which, carefully selecting wisdom and genius from the great wilderness of society, as the bee selects honey from the flowers of the thorn and the nettle, bound all human excellence in a chain, which, if it had not been prematurely broken, would have commanded opinion, and regenerated the world."

Scythrop proceeded to meditate on the practicability of reviving a confederation of regenerators. To get a clear view of his own ideas, and to feel the pulse of the wisdom and genius of the age, he wrote and published a treatise, in which his meanings were carefully wrapped up in the monk's hood of transcendental technology, but filled with hints of matter deep and dangerous, which he thought would set the whole nation in a ferment; and he awaited the result in awful expectation, as a miner who has fired a train awaits the explosion of a rock. However, he listened and heard nothing; for the explosion, if any ensued, was not sufficiently loud to shake a single leaf of the ivy on the towers of Nightmare Abbey; and some months afterwards he received a letter from his bookseller, informing him that only seven copies had been sold, and concluding with a polite request for the balance.

Scythrop did not despair. "Seven copies," he thought, "have been sold. Seven is a mystical number, and the omen is good. Let me find the seven purchasers of my seven copies, and they shall be the seven golden candlesticks with which I will illuminate the world."

Scythrop had a certain portion of mechanical genius, which his romantic projects tended to develop. He constructed models of cells and recesses, sliding panels and secret passages, that would have baffled the skill of the Parisian police. He took the opportunity of his father's absence to smuggle a dumb carpenter into the Abbey, and between them they gave reality to one of these models in Scythrop's tower. Scythrop foresaw that a great leader of human regeneration would be involved in fearful dilemmas, and determined, for the benefit of mankind in general, to adopt all possible precautions for the preservation of himself.

The servants, even the women, had been tutored into silence. Profound stillness reigned throughout and around the Abbey, except when the occasional shutting of a door would peal in long reverberations through the galleries, or the heavy tread of the pensive butler would wake the hollow echoes of the hall. Scythrop stalked about like the grand inquisitor, and the servants flitted past him like familiars. In his evening meditations on the terrace, under the ivy of the ruined tower, the only sounds that came to his ear were the rustling of the wind in the ivy, the plaintive voices of the feathered choristers, the owls, the occasional striking of the Abbey clock, and the monotonous dash of the sea on its low and level shore. In the meantime, he drank Madeira, and laid deep schemes for a thorough repair of the crazy fabric of human nature.

Chapter III

Mr. Glowry returned from London with the loss of his lawsuit. Justice was with him, but the law was against him. He found Scythrop in a mood most sympathetically tragic; and they vied with each other in enlivening their cups by lamenting the depravity of this degenerate age, and occasionally interspersing divers grim jokes about graves, worms, and epitaphs. Mr. Glowry's friends, whom we have mentioned in the first chapter, availed themselves of his return to pay him a simultaneous visit. At the same time arrived Scythrop's friend and fellow-collegian, the Honorable Mr. Listless. Mr. Glowry had discovered this fashionable young gentleman in London, "stretched on the rack of a too easy chair," and devoured with a gloomy and misanthropical nil curo, and had pressed him so earnestly to take the benefit of the pure country air, at Nightmare Abbey, that Mr. Listless, finding it would give him more trouble to refuse than to comply, summoned his French valet, Fatout, and told him he was going to Lincolnshire. On this simple hint, Fatout went to work, and the imperials were packed, and the post-chariot was at the door, without the Honorable Mr. Listless having said or thought another syllable on the subject.

Mr. and Mrs. Hilary brought with them an orphan niece, a daughter of Mr. Glowry's youngest sister, who had made a runaway love-match with an Irish officer. The lady's fortune disappeared in the first year: love, by a natural consequence, disappeared in the second: the Irishman himself, by a still more natural consequence, disappeared in the third. Mr. Glowry had allowed his sister an annuity, and she had lived in retirement with her only daughter, whom, at her death, which had recently happened, she commended to the care of Mrs. Hilary.

Miss Marionetta Celestina O'Carroll was a very blooming and accomplished young lady. Being a compound of the Allegro Vivace of the O'Carrolls, and of the Andante Doloroso of the Glowries, she exhibited in her own character all the diversities of an April sky. Her hair was light brown; her eyes hazel, and sparkling with a mild but fluctuating light; her features regular; her lips full, and of equal size; and her person surpassingly graceful. She was a proficient in music. Her conversation was sprightly, but always on subjects light in their nature and limited in their interest: for moral sympathies, in any general sense, had no place in her mind. She had some coquetry, and more caprice, liking and disliking almost in the same moment; pursuing an object with earnestness while it seemed unattainable, and rejecting it when in her power as not worth the trouble of possession.

Whether she was touched with a penchant for her cousin Scythrop, or was merely curious to see what effect the tender passion would have on so outré a person, she had not been three days in the Abbey before she threw out all the lures of her beauty and accomplishments to make a prize of his heart. Scythrop proved an easy conquest. The image of Miss Emily

Girouette was already sufficiently dimmed by the power of philosophy and the exercise of reason: for to these influences, or to any influence but the true one, are usually ascribed the mental cures performed by the great physician Time. Scythrop's romantic dreams had indeed given him many pure anticipated cognitions of combinations of beauty and intelligence, which, he had some misgivings, were not exactly realized in his cousin Marionetta; but, in spite of these misgivings, he soon became distractedly in love; which, when the young lady clearly perceived, she altered her tactics, and assumed as much coldness and reserve as she had before shown ardent and ingenuous attachment. Scythrop was confounded at the sudden change; but, instead of falling at her feet and requesting an explanation, he retreated to his tower, muffled himself in his nightcap, seated himself in the president's chair of his imaginary secret tribunal, summoned Marionetta with all terrible formalities, frightened her out of her wits, disclosed himself, and clasped the beautiful penitent to his bosom.

While he was acting this reverie — in the moment in which the awful president of the secret tribunal was throwing back his cowl and his mantle, and discovering himself to the lovely culprit as her adoring and magnanimous lover, the door of the study opened, and the real Marionetta appeared.

The motives which had led her to the tower were a little penitence, a little concern, a little affection, and a little fear as to what the sudden secession of Scythrop, occasioned by her sudden change of manner, might portend. She had tapped several times unheard, and of course unanswered; and at length, timidly and cautiously opening the door, she discovered him standing up before a black velvet chair, which was mounted on an old oak table, in the act of throwing open his striped

calico dressing gown, and flinging away his nightcap
— which is what the French call an imposing attitude.

Each stood a few moments fixed in their respective
places — the lady in astonishment, and the gentleman
in confusion. Marionetta was the first to break silence.
"For heaven's sake," said she, "my dear Scythrop, what
is the matter?"

"For heaven's sake, indeed!" said Scythrop, springing
from the table; "for your sake, Marionetta, and you are
my heaven, — distraction is the matter. I adore you,
Marionetta, and your cruelty drives me mad." He
threw himself at her knees, devoured her hand with
kisses, and breathed a thousand vows in the most
passionate language of romance.

Marionetta listened a long time in silence, till her
lover had exhausted his eloquence and paused for a
reply. She then said, with a very arch look, "I prithee
deliver thyself like a man of this world." The levity of
this quotation, and of the manner in which it was
delivered, jarred so discordantly on the high-wrought
enthusiasm of the romantic inamorato, that he sprang
upon his feet, and beat his forehead with his clenched
fist. The young lady was terrified; and, deeming it
expedient to soothe him, took one of his hands in hers,
placed the other hand on his shoulder, looked up in
his face with a winning seriousness, and said, in the
tenderest possible tone, "What would you have,
Scythrop?"

Scythrop was in heaven again. "What would I have?
What but you, Marionetta? You, for the companion of
my studies, the partner of my thoughts, the auxiliary
of my great designs for the emancipation of mankind."

"I am afraid I should be but a poor auxiliary,
Scythrop. What would you have me do?"

"Do as Rosalia does with Carlos, divine Marionetta.
Let us each open a vein in the other's arm, mix our

blood in a bowl, and drink it as a sacrament of love. Then we shall see visions of transcendental illumination, and soar on the wings of ideas into the space of pure intelligence."

Marionetta could not reply; she had not so strong a stomach as Rosalia, and turned sick at the proposition. She disengaged herself suddenly from Scythrop, sprang through the door of the tower, and fled with precipitation along the corridors. Scythrop pursued her, crying, "Stop, stop, Marionetta — my life, my love!" and was gaining rapidly on her flight, when, at an ill-omened corner, where two corridors ended in an angle, at the head of a staircase, he came into sudden and violent contact with Mr. Toobad, and they both plunged together to the foot of the stairs, like two billiard-balls into one pocket. This gave the young lady time to escape, and enclose herself in her chamber; while Mr. Toobad, rising slowly, and rubbing his knees and shoulders, said, "You see, my dear Scythrop, in this little incident, one of the innumerable proofs of the temporary supremacy of the devil; for what but a systematic design and concurrent contrivance of evil could have made the angles of time and place coincide in our unfortunate persons at the head of this accursed staircase?"

"Nothing else, certainly," said Scythrop: "you are perfectly in the right, Mr. Toobad. Evil, and mischief, and misery, and confusion, and vanity, and vexation of spirit, and death, and disease, and assassination, and war, and poverty, and pestilence, and famine, and avarice, and selfishness, and rancor, and jealousy, and spleen, and malevolence, and the disappointments of philanthropy, and the faithlessness of friendship, and the crosses of love — all prove the accuracy of your views, and the truth of your system; and it is not impossible that the infernal interruption of this fall downstairs may throw a color of evil on the whole of my future existence."

"My dear boy," said Mr. Toobad, "you have a fine eye for consequences."

So saying, he embraced Scythrop, who retired, with a disconsolate step, to dress for dinner; while Mr. Toobad stalked across the hall, repeating, "Woe to the inhabiters of the earth, and of the sea, for the devil is come among you, having great wrath."

Chapter IV

The flight of Marionetta, and the pursuit of Scythrop, had been witnessed by Mr. Glowry, who, in consequence, narrowly observed his son and his niece in the evening; and, concluding from their manner, that there was a better understanding between them than he wished to see, he determined on obtaining the next morning from Scythrop a full and satisfactory explanation. He, therefore, shortly after breakfast, entered Scythrop's tower, with a very grave face, and said, without ceremony or preface, "So, sir, you are in love with your cousin."

Scythrop, with as little hesitation, answered, "Yes, sir."

"That is candid, at least; and she is in love with you."

"I wish she were, sir."

"You know she is, sir."

"Indeed, sir, I do not."

"But you hope she is."

"I do, from my soul."

"Now that is very provoking, Scythrop, and very disappointing: I could not have supposed that you, Scythrop Glowry, of Nightmare Abbey, would have been infatuated with such a dancing, laughing, singing, thoughtless, careless, merry-hearted thing, as Marionetta — in all respects the reverse of you and me. It is very disappointing, Scythrop. And do you know, sir, that Marionetta has no fortune?"

"It is the more reason, sir, that her husband should have one."

"The more reason for her; but not for you. My wife had no fortune, and I had no consolation in my calamity. And do you reflect, sir, what an enormous slice this lawsuit has cut out of our family estate? we who used to be the greatest landed proprietors in Lincolnshire."

"To be sure, sir, we had more acres of fen than any man on this coast: but what are fens to love? What are dykes and windmills to Marionetta?"

"And what, sir, is love to a windmill? Not grist, I am certain: besides, sir, I have made a choice for you. I have made a choice for you, Scythrop. Beauty, genius, accomplishments, and a great fortune into the bargain. Such a lovely, serious creature, in a fine state of high dissatisfaction with the world, and everything in it. Such a delightful surprise I had prepared for you. Sir, I have pledged my honor to the contract — the honor of the Glowries of Nightmare Abbey: and now, sir, what is to be done?"

"Indeed, sir, I cannot say. I claim, on this occasion, that liberty of action which is the co-natal prerogative of every rational being."

"Liberty of action, sir? there is no such thing as liberty of action. We are all slaves and puppets of a blind and unpathetic necessity."

"Very true, sir; but liberty of action, between individuals, consists in their being differently influenced, or modified, by the same universal necessity; so that the results are unconsentaneous, and their respective necessitated volitions clash and fly off in a tangent."

"Your logic is good, sir: but you are aware, too, that one individual may be a medium of adhibiting to another a mode or form of necessity, which may have more or less influence in the production of consentaneity; and, therefore, sir, if you do not comply with my wishes in this instance (you have had your own way in everything else), I shall be under the necessity of disinheriting you, though I shall do it with tears in my eyes." Having said these words, he vanished suddenly, in the dread of Scythrop's logic.

Mr. Glowry immediately sought Mrs. Hilary, and communicated to her his views of the case in point. Mrs. Hilary, as the phrase is, was as fond of Marionetta as if she had been her own child: but — there is always a but on these occasions — she could do nothing for her in the way of fortune, as she had two hopeful sons, who were finishing their education at Brazen-nose, and who would not like to encounter any diminution of their prospects, when they should be brought out of the house of mental bondage — i.e. the university — to the land flowing with milk and honey — i.e. the west end of London.

Mrs. Hilary hinted to Marionetta, that propriety, and delicacy, and decorum, and dignity, &c. &c. &c.,* would require them to leave the Abbey immediately. Marionetta listened in silent submission, for she knew that her inheritance was passive obedience; but, when Scythrop, who had watched the opportunity of Mrs. Hilary's departure, entered, and, without speaking a word, threw himself at her feet in a paroxysm of grief, the young lady, in equal silence and sorrow, threw her arms round his neck and burst into tears. A very tender scene ensued, which the sympathetic susceptibilities of

---

* We are not masters of the whole vocabulary. See any novel by any literary lady.

the soft-hearted reader can more accurately imagine than we can delineate. But when Marionetta hinted that she was to leave the Abbey immediately, Scythrop snatched from its repository his ancestor's skull, filled it with Madeira, and presenting himself before Mr. Glowry, threatened to drink off the contents if Mr. Glowry did not immediately promise that Marionetta should not be taken from the Abbey without her own consent. Mr. Glowry, who took the Madeira to be some deadly brewage, gave the required promise in dismal panic. Scythrop returned to Marionetta with a joyful heart, and drank the Madeira by the way.

Mr. Glowry, during his residence in London, had come to an agreement with his friend Mr. Toobad, that a match between Scythrop and Mr. Toobad's daughter would be a very desirable occurrence. She was finishing her education in a German convent, but Mr. Toobad described her as being fully impressed with the truth of his Ahrimanic philosophy, and being altogether as gloomy and antithalian a young lady as Mr. Glowry himself could desire for the future mistress of Nightmare Abbey. She had a great fortune in her own right, which was not, as we have seen, without its weight in inducing Mr. Glowry to set his heart upon her as his daughter-in-law that was to be; he was therefore very much disturbed by Scythrop's untoward attachment to Marionetta. He condoled on the occasion with Mr. Toobad; who said, that he had been too long accustomed to the intermeddling of the devil in all his affairs, to be astonished at this new trace of his cloven claw; but that he hoped to outwit him yet, for he was sure there could be no comparison between his daughter and Marionetta in the mind of any one who had a proper perception of the fact, that, the world being a great theater of evil, seriousness and solemnity are the characteristics of wisdom, and laughter and merriment make a human being no better than a baboon. Mr. Glowry comforted himself with this view of the subject, and urged Mr. Toobad to expedite his daughter's return from Germany. Mr. Toobad said he was in daily expectation of her arrival in London, and would set off immediately to meet her, that he might lose no time in bringing her to Nightmare Abbey. "Then," he added, "we shall see whether Thalia or Melpomene — whether the Allegra or the Penserosa — will carry off the symbol of victory."

"There can be no doubt," said Mr. Glowry, "which way the scale will incline, or Scythrop is no true scion of the venerable stem of the Glowries."

Chapter V

Marionetta felt secure of Scythrop's heart; and not-withstanding the difficulties that surrounded her, she could not debar herself from the pleasure of torment-ing her lover, whom she kept in a perpetual fever. Sometimes she would meet him with the most unquali-fied affection; sometimes with the most chilling indif-ference; rousing him to anger by artificial coldness — softening him to love by eloquent tenderness — or inflaming him to jealousy by coquetting with the Hon-orable Mr. Listless, who seemed, under her magical influence, to burst into sudden life, like the bud of the evening primrose. Sometimes she would sit by the piano, and listen with becoming attention to Scythrop's pathetic remonstrances; but, in the most impassioned part of his oratory, she would convert all his ideas into a chaos, by striking up some Rondo Allegro, and saying, "Is it not pretty?" Scythrop would begin to storm; and she would answer him with,

"Zitti, zitti, piano, piano,
    Non facciamo confusione,"

or some similar facezia, till he would start away from her, and enclose himself in his tower, in an agony of agitation, vowing to renounce her, and her whole sex, forever; and returning to her presence at the summons of the billet, which she never failed to send with many expressions of penitence and promises of amendment. Scythrop's schemes for regenerating the world, and detecting his seven golden candlesticks, went on very slowly in this fever of his spirit.

Things proceeded in this train for several days; and Mr. Glowry began to be uneasy at receiving no intelligence from Mr. Toobad; when one evening the latter rushed into the library, where the family and the visitors were assembled, vociferating, "The devil is come among you, having great wrath!" He then drew Mr. Glowry aside into another apartment, and after remaining some time together, they reentered the library with faces of great dismay, but did not condescend to explain to any one the cause of their discomfiture.

The next morning, early, Mr. Toobad departed. Mr. Glowry sighed and groaned all day, and said not a word to any one. Scythrop had quarreled, as usual, with Marionetta, and was enclosed in his tower, in a fit of morbid sensibility. Marionetta was comforting herself at the piano, with singing the airs of Nina pazza per amore; and the Honorable Mr. Listless was listening to the harmony, as he lay supine on the sofa, with a book in his hand, into which he peeped at intervals. The Reverend Mr. Larynx approached the sofa, and proposed a game at billiards.

THE HONORABLE MR. LISTLESS

Billiards! Really I should be very happy; but, in my present exhausted state, the exertion is too much for me. I do not know when I have been equal to such an effort. (*He rang the bell for his valet. Fatout entered.*)

Fatout! when did I play at billiards last?

FATOUT
De fourteen December de last year, Monsieur. (*Fatout bowed and retired.*)

THE HONORABLE MR. LISTLESS
So it was. Seven months ago. You see, Mr. Larynx; you see, sir. My nerves, Miss O'Carroll, my nerves are shattered. I have been advised to try Bath. Some of the faculty recommend Cheltenham. I think of trying both, as the seasons don't clash. The season, you know, Mr. Larynx — the season, Miss O'Carroll — the season is everything.

MARIONETTA
And health is something. N'est-ce pas, Mr. Larynx?

THE REVEREND MR. LARYNX
Most assuredly, Miss O'Carroll. For, however reasoners may dispute about the summum bonum, none of them will deny that a very good dinner is a very good thing: and what is a good dinner without a good appetite? and whence is a good appetite but from good health? Now, Cheltenham, Mr. Listless, is famous for good appetites.

THE HONORABLE MR. LISTLESS
The best piece of logic I ever heard, Mr. Larynx; the very best, I assure you. I have thought very seriously of Cheltenham: very seriously and profoundly. I thought of it — let me see — when did I think of it? (*He rang again, and Fatout reappeared.*) Fatout! when did I think of going to Cheltenham, and did not go?

FATOUT
De Juillet twenty-von, de last summer, Monsieur. (*Fatout retired.*)

THE HONORABLE MR. LISTLESS
So it was. An invaluable fellow that, Mr. Larynx — invaluable, Miss O'Carroll.

MARIONETTA
So I should judge, indeed. He seems to serve you as a walking memory, and to be a living chronicle, not of your actions only, but of your thoughts.

THE HONORABLE MR. LISTLESS
An excellent definition of the fellow, Miss O'Carroll, excellent, upon my honor. Ha! ha! he! Heigho! Laughter is pleasant, but the exertion is too much for me.

A parcel was brought in for Mr. Listless; it had been sent express. Fatout was summoned to unpack it; and it proved to contain a new novel, and a new poem, both of which had long been anxiously expected by the whole host of fashionable readers; and the last number of a popular Review, of which the editor and his coadjutors were in high favor at court, and enjoyed ample pensions for their services to church and state. As Fatout left the room, Mr. Flosky entered, and curiously inspected the literary arrivals.

MR. FLOSKY
(*Turning over the leaves.*) "Devilman, a novel." Hm. Hatred — revenge — misanthropy — and quotations from the Bible. Hm. This is the morbid anatomy of black bile. — "Paul Jones, a poem." Hm. I see how it is. Paul Jones, an amiable enthusiast — disappointed

in his affections — turns pirate from ennui and magnanimity — cuts various masculine throats, wins various feminine hearts — is hanged at the yard-arm! The catastrophe is very awkward, and very unpoetical. — "The Downing Street Review." Hm. First article — An Ode to the Red Book, by Roderick Sackbut, Esquire. Hm. His own poem reviewed by himself. Hm-m-m.

(*Mr. Flosky proceeded in silence to look over the other articles of the review; Marionetta inspected the novel, and Mr. Listless the poem.*)

THE REVEREND MR. LARYNX
For a young man of fashion and family, Mr. Listless, you seem to be of a very studious turn.

THE HONORABLE MR. LISTLESS
Studious! You are pleased to be facetious, Mr. Larynx. I hope you do not suspect me of being studious. I have finished my education. But there are some fashionable books that one must read, because they are ingredients of the talk of the day; otherwise, I am no fonder of books than I dare say you yourself are, Mr. Larynx.

THE REVEREND MR. LARYNX
Why, sir, I cannot say that I am indeed particularly fond of books; yet neither can I say that I never do read. A tale or a poem, now and then, to a circle of ladies over their work, is no very heterodox employment of the vocal energy. And I must say, for myself, that few men have a more Joblike endurance of the eternally recurring questions and answers that interweave themselves, on these occasions, with the crisis of an adventure, and heighten the distress of a tragedy.

THE HONORABLE MR. LISTLESS
And very often make the distress when the author
has omitted it.

MARIONETTA
I shall try your patience some rainy morning, Mr.
Larynx; and Mr. Listless shall recommend us the very
newest new book, that everybody reads.

THE HONORABLE MR. LISTLESS
You shall receive it, Miss O'Carroll, with all the gloss
of novelty; fresh as a ripe green-gage in all the downi-
ness of its bloom. A mail-coach copy from Edinburgh,
forwarded express from London.

MR. FLOSKY
This rage for novelty is the bane of literature. Except
my works and those of my particular friends, nothing
is good that is not as old as Jeremy Taylor: and, *entre
nous,* the best parts of my friends' books were either
written or suggested by myself.

THE HONORABLE MR. LISTLESS
Sir, I reverence you. But I must say, modern books
are very consolatory and congenial to my feelings.
There is, as it were, a delightful northeast wind, an
intellectual blight breathing through them; a delicious
misanthropy and discontent, that demonstrates the
nullity of virtue and energy, and puts me in good
humor with myself and my sofa.

MR. FLOSKY
Very true, sir. Modern literature is a northeast wind
— a blight of the human soul. I take credit to myself
for having helped to make it so. The way to produce
fine fruit is to blight the flower. You call this a paradox.

Marry, so be it. Ponder thereon.

The conversation was interrupted by the reappearance of Mr. Toobad, covered with mud. He just showed himself at the door, muttered "The devil is come among you!" and vanished. The road which connected Nightmare Abbey with the civilized world, was artificially raised above the level of the fens, and ran through them in a straight line as far as the eye could reach, with a ditch on each side, of which the water was rendered invisible by the aquatic vegetation that covered the surface. Into one of these ditches the sudden action of a shy horse, which took fright at a windmill, had precipitated the traveling chariot of Mr. Toobad, who had been reduced to the necessity of scrambling in dismal plight through the window. One of the wheels was found to be broken; and Mr. Toobad, leaving the postilion to get the chariot as well as he could to Claydyke for the purpose of cleaning and repairing, had walked back to Nightmare Abbey, followed by his servant with the imperial, and repeating all the way his favorite quotation from the Revelations.

Chapter VI

Mr. Toobad had found his daughter Celinda in London, and after the first joy of meeting was over, told her he had a husband ready for her. The young lady replied, very gravely, that she should take the liberty to choose for herself. Mr. Toobad said he saw the devil was determined to interfere with all his projects, but he was resolved on his own part, not to have on his conscience the crime of passive obedience and non-resistance to Lucifer, and therefore she should marry the person he had chosen for her. Miss Toobad replied, très posément, she assuredly would not. "Celinda, Celinda," said Mr. Toobad, "you most assuredly shall." — "Have I not a fortune in my own right, sir?" said Celinda. "The more is the pity," said Mr. Toobad: "but I can find means, miss; I can find means. There are more ways than one of breaking in obstinate girls." They parted for the night with the expression of opposite resolutions, and in the morning the young lady's chamber was found empty, and what was become of her Mr. Toobad had no clue to conjecture. He continued to investigate town and country in search of her; visiting and revisiting Nightmare Abbey at intervals, to consult with his friend, Mr. Glowry. Mr. Glowry agreed with Mr. Toobad that this was a very flagrant instance of filial disobedience and rebellion; and Mr. Toobad declared, that when he discovered the fugitive, she should find that "the devil was come unto her, having great wrath."

In the evening, the whole party met, as usual, in the library. Marionetta sat at the harp; the Honorable Mr. Listless sat by her and turned over her music, though the exertion was almost too much for him. The Reverend Mr. Larynx relieved him occasionally in this delightful labor. Scythrop, tormented by the demon Jealousy, sat in the corner biting his lips and fingers. Marionetta looked at him every now and then with a smile of most provoking good humor, which he pretended not to see, and which only the more exasperated his troubled spirit. He took down a volume of Dante, and pretended to be deeply interested in the Purgatorio, though he knew not a word he was reading, as Marionetta was well aware; who, tripping across the room, peeped into his book, and said to him, "I see you are in the middle of Purgatory." — "I am in the middle of hell," said Scythrop furiously. "Are you?" said she; "then come across the room, and I will sing you the finale of Don Giovanni."

"Let me alone," said Scythrop. Marionetta looked at him with a deprecating smile, and said, "You unjust, cross creature, you." — "Let me alone," said Scythrop, but much less emphatically than at first, and by no means wishing to be taken at his word. Marionetta left him immediately, and returning to the harp, said, just loud enough for Scythrop to hear — "Did you ever read Dante, Mr. Listless? Scythrop is reading Dante, and is just now in Purgatory." — "And I," said the Honorable Mr. Listless, "am not reading Dante, and am just now in Paradise," bowing to Marionetta.

MARIONETTA
You are very gallant, Mr. Listless; and I dare say you are very fond of reading Dante.

THE HONORABLE MR. LISTLESS
I don't know how it is, but Dante never came in my way till lately. I never had him in my collection, and if I had had him I should not have read him. But I find he is growing fashionable, and I am afraid I must read him some wet morning.

MARIONETTA
No, read him some evening, by all means. Were you ever in love, Mr. Listless?

THE HONORABLE MR. LISTLESS
I assure you, Miss O'Carroll, never — till I came to Nightmare Abbey. I dare say it is very pleasant; but it seems to give so much trouble that I fear the exertion would be too much for me.

MARIONETTA
Shall I teach you a compendious method of courtship, that will give you no trouble whatever?

THE HONORABLE MR. LISTLESS
You will confer on me an inexpressible obligation. I am all impatience to learn it.

MARIONETTA
Sit with your back to the lady and read Dante; only be sure to begin in the middle, and turn over three or four pages at once — backwards as well as forwards, and she will immediately perceive that you are desperately in love with her — desperately.

(*The Honorable Mr. Listless sitting between Scythrop and*

Marionetta, and fixing all his attention on the beautiful speaker, did not observe Scythrop, who was doing as she described.)

THE HONORABLE MR. LISTLESS
You are pleased to be facetious, Miss O'Carroll. The lady would infallibly conclude that I was the greatest brute in town.

MARIONETTA
Far from it. She would say, perhaps, some people have odd methods of showing their affection.

THE HONORABLE MR. LISTLESS
But I should think, with submission —

MR. FLOSKY
(Joining them from another part of the room.)
Did I not hear Mr. Listless observe that Dante is becoming fashionable?

THE HONORABLE MR. LISTLESS
I did hazard a remark to that effect, Mr. Flosky, though I speak on such subjects with a consciousness of my own nothingness, in the presence of so great a man as Mr. Flosky. I know not what is the color of Dante's devils, but as he is certainly becoming fashionable I conclude they are blue; for the blue devils, as it seems to me, Mr. Flosky, constitute the fundamental feature of fashionable literature.

MR. FLOSKY
The blue are, indeed, the staple commodity; but as they will not always be commanded, the black, red, and grey may be admitted as substitutes. Tea, late dinners, and the French Revolution, have played the devil, Mr.

Listless, and brought the devil into play.

MR. TOOBAD (*starting up*)
Having great wrath.

MR. FLOSKY
This is no play upon words, but the sober sadness of veritable fact.

THE HONORABLE MR. LISTLESS
Tea, late dinners, and the French Revolution. I cannot exactly see the connection of ideas.

MR. FLOSKY
I should be sorry if you could; I pity the man who can see the connection of his own ideas. Still more do I pity him, the connection of whose ideas any other person can see. Sir, the great evil is, that there is too much commonplace light in our moral and political literature; and light is a great enemy to mystery, and mystery is a great friend to enthusiasm. Now the enthusiasm for abstract truth is an exceedingly fine thing, as long as the truth, which is the object of the enthusiasm, is so completely abstract as to be altogether out of the reach of the human faculties; and, in that sense, I have myself an enthusiasm for truth, but in no other, for the pleasure of metaphysical investigation lies in the means, not in the end; and if the end could be found, the pleasure of the means would cease. The mind, to be kept in health, must be kept in exercise. The proper exercise of the mind is elaborate reasoning. Analytical reasoning is a base and mechanical process, which takes to pieces and examines, bit by bit, the rude material of knowledge, and extracts therefrom a few hard and obstinate things called facts, everything in the shape of which I cordially hate. But synthetical

reasoning, setting up as its goal some unattainable abstraction, like an imaginary quantity in algebra, and commencing its course with taking for granted some two assertions which cannot be proved, from the union of these two assumed truths produces a third assumption, and so on in infinite series, to the unspeakable benefit of the human intellect. The beauty of this process is, that at every step it strikes out into two branches, in a compound ratio of ramification; so that you are perfectly sure of losing your way, and keeping your mind in perfect health, by the perpetual exercise of an interminable quest; and for these reasons I have christened my eldest son Emanuel Kant Flosky.

THE REVEREND MR. LARYNX
Nothing can be more luminous.

THE HONORABLE MR. LISTLESS
And what has all that to do with Dante, and the blue devils?

MR. HILARY
Not much, I should think, with Dante, but a great deal with the blue devils.

MR. FLOSKY
It is very certain, and much to be rejoiced at, that our literature is hag-ridden. Tea has shattered our nerves; late dinners make us slaves of indigestion; the French Revolution has made us shrink from the name of philosophy, and has destroyed, in the more refined part of the community (of which number I am one), all enthusiasm for political liberty. That part of the reading public which shuns the solid food of reason for the light diet of fiction, requires a perpetual adhibition of sauce piquante to the palate of its depraved

imagination. It lived upon ghosts, goblins, and skeletons (I and my friend Mr. Sackbut served up a few of the best), till even the devil himself, though magnified to the size of Mount Athos, became too base, common, and popular, for its surfeited appetite. The ghosts have therefore been laid, and the devil has been cast into outer darkness, and now the delight of our spirits is to dwell on all the vices and blackest passions of our nature, tricked out in a masquerade dress of heroism and disappointed benevolence; the whole secret of which lies in forming combinations that contradict all our experience, and affixing the purple shred of some particular virtue to that precise character, in which we should be most certain not to find it in the living world; and making this single virtue not only redeem all the real and manifest vices of the character, but make them actually pass for necessary adjuncts, and indispensable accompaniments and characteristics of the said virtue.

MR. TOOBAD

That is, because the devil is come among us, and finds it for his interest to destroy all our perceptions of the distinctions of right and wrong.

MARIONETTA

I do not precisely enter into your meaning, Mr. Flosky, and should be glad if you would make it a little more plain to me.

MR. FLOSKY

One or two examples will do it, Miss O'Carroll. If I were to take all the mean and sordid qualities of a money-dealing Jew, and tack on to them, as with a nail, the quality of extreme benevolence, I should have a very decent hero for a modern novel; and should contribute my quota to the fashionable method of administering a mass of vice, under a thin and unnatural covering of virtue, like a spider wrapped in a bit of gold leaf, and administered as a wholesome pill. On the same principle, if a man knocks me down, and takes my purse and watch by main force, I turn him to account, and set him forth in a tragedy as a dashing young fellow, disinherited for his romantic generosity, and full of a most amiable hatred of the world in general, and his own country in particular, and of a most enlightened and chivalrous affection for himself: then, with the addition of a wild girl to fall in love with him, and a series of adventures in which they break all the Ten Commandments in succession (always, you will observe, for some sublime motive, which must be carefully analyzed in its progress), I have as amiable a pair of tragic characters as ever issued from that new region of the *belles lettres,* which I have called the Morbid Anatomy of Black Bile, and which is greatly to be admired and rejoiced at, as affording a fine scope for the exhibition of mental power.

MR. HILARY

Which is about as well employed as the power of a hothouse would be in forcing up a nettle to the size of an elm. If we go on in this way, we shall have a new art of poetry, of which one of the first rules will be: To remember to forget that there are any such things as sunshine and music in the world.

THE HONORABLE MR. LISTLESS

It seems to be the case with us at present, or we should not have interrupted Miss O'Carroll's music with this exceedingly dry conversation.

MR. FLOSKY

I should be most happy if Miss O'Carroll would remind us that there are yet both music and sunshine —

THE HONORABLE MR. LISTLESS

In the voice and the smile of beauty. May I entreat the favor of — (*turning over the pages of music.*)
All were silent, and Marionetta sung: —

Why are thy looks so blank, grey friar?
    Why are thy looks so blue?
Thou seem'st more pale and lank, grey friar,
Than thou wast used to do:
    Say, what has made thee rue?
Thy form was plump, and a light did shine
    In thy round and ruby face,
Which showed an outward visible sign
    Of an inward spiritual grace: —
    Say, what has changed thy case?
Yet will I tell thee true, grey friar,
    I very well can see,
That, if thy looks are blue, grey friar,
    'Tis all for love of me, —
    'Tis all for love of me.
But breathe not thy vows to me, grey friar,
    Oh, breathe them not, I pray;
For ill beseems in a reverend friar,
    The love of a mortal may;
    And I needs must say thee nay.
But, could'st thou think my heart to move
    With that pale and silent scowl,
Know, he who would win a maiden's love,
    Whether clad in cap or cowl,
    Must be more of a lark than an owl.

Scythrop immediately replaced Dante on the shelf, and joined the circle round the beautiful singer.

Marionetta gave him a smile of approbation that fully restored his complacency, and they continued on the best possible terms during the remainder of the evening. The Honorable Mr. Listless turned over the leaves with double alacrity, saying, "You are severe upon invalids, Miss O'Carroll: to escape your satire, I must try to be sprightly, though the exertion is too much for me."

Chapter VII

A new visitor arrived at the Abbey, in the person of Mr. Asterias, the ichthyologist. This gentleman had passed his life in seeking the living wonders of the deep through the four quarters of the world; he had a cabinet of stuffed and dried fishes, of shells, seaweeds, corals, and madrepores, that was the admiration and envy of the Royal Society. He had penetrated into the watery den of the Sepia Octopus, disturbed the conjugal happiness of that turtle-dove of the ocean, and come off victorious in a sanguinary conflict. He had been becalmed in the tropical seas, and had watched, in eager expectation, though unhappily always in vain, to see the colossal polypus rise from the water, and entwine its enormous arms round the masts and the rigging. He maintained the origin of all things from water, and insisted that the polypodes were the first of animated things, and that, from their round bodies and many-shooting arms, the Hindus had taken their gods, the most ancient of deities. But the chief object of his ambition, the end and aim of his researches, was to discover a triton and a mermaid, the existence of which he most potently and implicitly believed, and was prepared to demonstrate, *a priori, a posteriori, a fortiori,* synthetically and analytically, syllogistically and inductively, by arguments deduced both from acknowledged facts and plausible hypotheses. A report that a mermaid had been seen 'sleeking her soft alluring locks' on the seacoast of Lincolnshire, had brought him in great haste from London, to pay a long-promised and often-postponed visit to his old acquaintance, Mr. Glowry.

Mr. Asterias was accompanied by his son, to whom he had given the name of Aquarius — flattering himself that he would, in the process of time, become a constellation among the stars of ichthyological science. What charitable female had lent him the mould in which this son was cast, no one pretended to know; and, as he never dropped the most distant allusion to Aquarius's mother, some of the wags of London maintained that he had received the favors of a mermaid, and that the scientific perquisitions which kept him always prowling about the seashore, were directed by the less philosophical motive of regaining his lost love.

Mr. Asterias perlustrated the seacoast for several days, and reaped disappointment, but not despair. One night, shortly after his arrival, he was sitting in one of the windows of the library, looking towards the sea, when his attention was attracted by a figure which was moving near the edge of the surf, and which was dimly visible through the moonless summer night. Its motions were irregular, like those of a person in a state of indecision. It had extremely long hair, which floated in the wind. Whatever else it might be, it certainly was not a fisherman. It might be a lady; but it was neither Mrs. Hilary nor Miss O'Carroll, for they were both in the library. It might be one of the female servants; but it had too much grace, and too striking an air of habitual liberty, to render it probable. Besides, what should one of the female servants be doing there at this hour, moving to and fro, as it seemed, without any visible purpose? It could scarcely be a stranger; for Claydyke, the nearest village, was ten miles distant; and what female would come ten miles across the fens, for no purpose but to hover over the surf under the walls of Nightmare Abbey? Might it not be a mermaid? It was possibly a mermaid. It was probably a mermaid. It was very probably a mermaid. Nay, what else could it be but a mermaid? It certainly was a mermaid. Mr. Asterias stole out of the library on tiptoe, with his finger on his lips, having beckoned Aquarius to follow him.

The rest of the party was in great surprise at Mr. Asterias's movement, and some of them approached the window to see if the locality would tend to elucidate the mystery. Presently they saw him and Aquarius cautiously stealing along on the other side of the moat, but they saw nothing more; and Mr. Asterias returning, told them, with accents of great disappointment, that he had had a glimpse of a mermaid, but she had eluded him in the darkness, and was gone, he presumed, to sup with some enamored triton, in a submarine grotto.

"But, seriously, Mr. Asterias," said the Honorable Mr. Listless, "do you positively believe there are such things as mermaids?"

MR. ASTERIAS
Most assuredly; and tritons too.

THE HONORABLE MR. LISTLESS
What! things that are half human and half fish?

MR. ASTERIAS
Precisely. They are the orangutans of the sea. But I am persuaded that there are also complete sea men, differing in no respect from us, but that they are stupid,

and covered with scales; for, though our organization seems to exclude us essentially from the class of amphibious animals, yet anatomists well know that the foramen ovale may remain open in an adult, and that respiration is, in that case, not necessary to life: and how can it be otherwise explained that the Indian divers, employed in the pearl fishery, pass whole hours under the water; and that the famous Swedish gardener of Troningholm lived a day and a half under the ice without being drowned? A Nereid, or mermaid, was taken in the year 1403 in a Dutch lake, and was in every respect like a French woman, except that she did not speak. Towards the end of the seventeenth century, an English ship, a hundred and fifty leagues from land, in the Greenland seas, discovered a flotilla of sixty or seventy little skiffs, in each of which was a triton, or sea man: at the approach of the English vessel the whole of them, seized with simultaneous fear, disappeared, skiffs and all, under the water, as if they had been a human variety of the nautilus. The illustrious Don Feijoo has preserved an authentic and well attested story of a young Spaniard, named Francis de la Vega, who, bathing with some of his friends in June, 1674, suddenly dived under the sea and rose no more. His friends thought him drowned; they were plebeians and pious Catholics; but a philosopher might very legitimately have drawn the same conclusion.

THE REVEREND MR. LARYNX
Nothing could be more logical.

MR. ASTERIAS
Five years afterwards, some fishermen near Cadiz found in their nets a triton, or sea man; they spoke to him in several languages —

THE REVEREND MR. LARYNX
They were very learned fishermen.

MR. HILARY
They had the gift of tongues by especial favor of their brother fisherman, Saint Peter.

THE HONORABLE MR. LISTLESS
Is Saint Peter the tutelar saint of Cadiz?

(None of the company could answer this question, and MR. ASTERIAS *proceeded.)*
They spoke to him in several languages, but he was as mute as a fish. They handed him over to some holy friars, who exorcised him; but the devil was mute too. After some days he pronounced the name Lierganes. A monk took him to that village. His mother and brothers recognized and embraced him; but he was as insensible to their caresses as any other fish would have been. He had some scales on his body, which dropped off by degrees; but his skin was as hard and rough as shagreen. He stayed at home nine years, without recovering his speech or his reason: he then disappeared again; and one of his old acquaintance, some years after, saw him pop his head out of the water near the coast of the Asturias. These facts were certified by his brothers, and by Don Gaspardo de la Riba Aguero, Knight of Saint James, who lived near Lierganes, and often had the pleasure of our triton's company to dinner. — Pliny mentions an embassy of the Olyssiponians to Tiberius, to give him intelligence of a triton which had been heard playing on its shell in a certain cave; with several other authenticated facts on the subject of tritons and Nereids.

THE HONORABLE MR. LISTLESS
You astonish me. I have been much on the seashore, in the season, but I do not think I ever saw a mermaid. (*He rang, and summoned Fatout, who made his appearance half-seas over.*) Fatout! did I ever see a mermaid?

FATOUT
Mermaid! mer-r-m-m-aid! Ah! merry maid! Oui, monsieur! Yes, sir, very many. I vish dere vas von or two here in de kitchen — ma foi! Dey be all as melancholic as so many tombstone.

THE HONORABLE MR. LISTLESS
I mean, Fatout, an odd kind of human fish.

FATOUT
De odd fish! Ah, oui! I understand de phrase: ve have seen nothing else since ve left town — ma foi!

THE HONORABLE MR. LISTLESS
You seem to have a cup too much, sir.

FATOUT
Non, monsieur: de cup too little. De fen be very unwholesome, and I drink-a-de ponch vid Raven de butler, to keep out de bad air.

THE HONORABLE MR. LISTLESS
Fatout! I insist on your being sober.

FATOUT
Oui, monsieur; I vil be as sober as de reverendissime pere Jean. I should be ver glad of de merry maid; but de butler be de odd fish, and he swim in de bowl de ponch. Ah! ah! I do recollect de leetle-a song: — "About fair maids, and about fair maids, and about my merry

maids all." (*Fatout reeled out, singing.*)

THE HONORABLE MR. LISTLESS

I am overwhelmed: I never saw the rascal in such a condition before. But will you allow me, Mr. Asterias, to inquire into the *cui bono* of all the pains and expense you have incurred to discover a mermaid? The *cui bono,* sir, is the question I always take the liberty to ask when I see any one taking much trouble for any object. I am myself a sort of Signor Pococurante, and should like to know if there be any thing better or pleasanter, than the state of existing and doing nothing.

MR. ASTERIAS

I have made many voyages, Mr. Listless, to remote and barren shores: I have traveled over desert and inhospitable lands: I have defied danger — I have endured fatigue — I have submitted to privation. In the midst of these I have experienced pleasures which I would not at any time have exchanged for that of existing and doing nothing. I have known many evils, but I have never known the worst of all, which, as it seems to me, are those which are comprehended in the inexhaustible varieties of ennui: spleen, chagrin, vapors, blue devils, time-killing, discontent, misanthropy, and all their interminable train of fretfulness, querulousness, suspicions, jealousies, and fears, which have alike infected society, and the literature of society; and which would make an arctic ocean of the human mind, if the more humane pursuits of philosophy and science did not keep alive the better feelings and more valuable energies of our nature.

THE HONORABLE MR. LISTLESS

You are pleased to be severe upon our fashionable *belles lettres.*

MR. ASTERIAS

Surely not without reason, when pirates, highway-
men, and other varieties of the extensive genus Ma-
rauder, are the only *beau ideal* of the active, as splenetic
and railing misanthropy is of the speculative energy.
A gloomy brow and a tragical voice seem to have been
of late the characteristics of fashionable manners: and
a morbid, withering, deadly, antisocial sirocco, loaded
with moral and political despair, breathes through all
the groves and valleys of the modern Parnassus; while
science moves on in the calm dignity of its course,
affording to youth delights equally pure and vivid to
maturity, calm and grateful occupation — to old age,
the most pleasing recollections and inexhaustible materials of agreeable and salutary reflection; and, while
its votary enjoys the disinterested pleasure of enlarging
the intellect and increasing the comforts of society, he
is himself independent of the caprices of human inter-
course and the accidents of human fortune. Nature is
his great and inexhaustible treasure. His days are always
too short for his enjoyment: ennui is a stranger to his
door. At peace with the world and with his own mind,
he suffices to himself, makes all around him happy,
and the close of his pleasing and beneficial existence
is the evening of a beautiful day

THE HONORABLE MR. LISTLESS

Really I should like very well to lead such a life
myself, but the exertion would be too much for me.
Besides, I have been at college. I contrive to get through
my day by sinking the morning in bed, and killing the
evening in company; dressing and dining in the inter-
mediate space, and stopping the chinks and crevices of
the few vacant moments that remain with a little easy
reading. And that amiable discontent and antisociality

which you reprobate in our present drawing room-table literature, I find, I do assure you, a very fine mental tonic, which reconciles me to my favorite pursuit of doing nothing, by showing me that nobody is worth doing any thing for.

MARIONETTA

But is there not in such compositions a kind of unconscious self-detection, which seems to carry their own antidote with them? For surely no one who cordially and truly either hates or despises the world will publish a volume every three months to say so.

MR. FLOSKY

There is a secret in all this, which I will elucidate with a dusky remark. According to Berkeley, the esse of things is percipi. They exist as they are perceived. But, leaving for the present, as far as relates to the material world, the materialists, hyloists, and antihyloists, to settle this point among them, which is indeed

A subtle question, raised among
Those out o' their wits, and those i' the wrong:

for only we transcendentalists are in the right: we may very safely assert that the esse of happiness is percipi. It exists as it is perceived. "It is the mind that maketh well or ill." The elements of pleasure and pain are every where. The degree of happiness that any circumstances or objects can confer on us depends on the mental disposition with which we approach them. If you consider what is meant by the common phrases, a happy disposition and a discontented temper, you will perceive that the truth for which I am contending is universally admitted.

(Mr. Flosky suddenly stopped: he found himself uninten-

tionally trespassing within the limits of common sense.)

MR. HILARY

It is very true, a happy disposition finds materials of enjoyment every where. In the city, or the country — in society, or in solitude — in the theater, or the forest — in the hum of the multitude, or in the silence of the mountains, are alike materials of reflection and elements of pleasure. It is one mode of pleasure to listen to the music of "Don Giovanni," in a theater glittering with light, and crowded with elegance and beauty: it is another to glide at sunset over the bosom of a lonely lake, where no sound disturbs the silence but the motion of the boat through the waters. A happy disposition derives pleasure from both, a discontented temper from neither, but is always busy in detecting deficiencies, and feeding dissatisfaction with comparisons. The one gathers all the flowers, the other all the nettles, in its path. The one has the faculty of enjoying everything, the other of enjoying nothing. The one realizes all the pleasure of the present good; the other converts it into pain, by pining after something better, which is only better because it is not present, and which, if it were present, would not be enjoyed. These morbid spirits are in life what professed critics are in literature; they see nothing but faults, because they are predetermined to shut their eyes to beauties. The critic does his utmost to blight genius in its infancy; that which rises in spite of him he will not see; and then he complains of the decline of literature. In like manner, these cankers of society complain of human nature and society, when they have willfully debarred themselves from all the good they contain, and done their utmost to blight their own happiness and that of all around them. Misanthropy is sometimes the product of disappointed benevolence; but it is more frequently the offspring of overweening and mortified vanity, quarrelling with the world for not being better treated than it deserves.

SCYTHROP (*to Marionetta*)

"These remarks are rather uncharitable. There is great good in human nature, but it is at present ill-conditioned. Ardent spirits cannot but be dissatisfied with things as they are; and, according to their views of the probabilities of amelioration, they will rush into the extremes of either hope or despair — of which the first is enthusiasm, and the second misanthropy; but their sources in this case are the same, as the Severn and the Wye run in different directions, and both rise in Plinlimmon.

MARIONETTA

"And there is salmon in both;" for the resemblance is about as close as that between Macedon and Monmouth.

Chapter VIII

Marionetta observed the next day a remarkable perturbation in Scythrop, for which she could not imagine any probable cause. She was willing to believe at first that it had some transient and trifling source, and would pass off in a day or two; but, contrary to this expectation, it daily increased. She was well aware that Scythrop had a strong tendency to the love of mystery, for its own sake; that is to say, he would employ mystery to serve a purpose, but would first choose his purpose by its capability of mystery. He seemed now to have more mystery on his hands than the laws of the system allowed, and to wear his coat of darkness with an air of great discomfort. All her little playful arts lost by degrees much of their power either to irritate or to soothe; and the first perception of her diminished influence produced in her an immediate depression of spirits, and a consequent sadness of demeanor, that rendered her very interesting to Mr. Glowry; who, duly considering the improbability of accomplishing his wishes with respect to Miss Toobad (which improbability naturally increased in the diurnal ratio of that young lady's absence), began to reconcile himself by degrees to the idea of Marionetta being his daughter.

Marionetta made many ineffectual attempts to extract from Scythrop the secret of his mystery; and, in despair of drawing it from himself, began to form hopes that she might find a clue to it from Mr. Flosky, who was Scythrop's dearest friend, and was more frequently than any other person admitted to his solitary tower. Mr. Flosky, however, had ceased to be visible in a morning He was engaged in the composition of a dismal ballad; and, Marionetta's uneasiness overcoming her scruples of decorum, she determined to seek him in the apartment which he had chosen for his study. She tapped at the door, and at the sound "Come in," entered the apartment. It was noon, and the sun was shining in full splendor, much to the annoyance of Mr. Flosky, who had obviated the inconvenience by closing the shutters, and drawing the window-curtains. He was sitting at his table by the light of a solitary candle, with a pen in one hand, and a muffineer in the other, with which he occasionally sprinkled salt on the wick, to make it burn blue. He sate with 'his eye in a fine frenzy rolling,' and turned his inspired gaze on Marionetta as if she had been the ghastly ladie of a magical vision; then placed his hand before his eyes, with an appearance of manifest pain — shook his head — withdrew his hand — rubbed his eyes, like a waking man — and said, in a tone of ruefulness most jeremi-taylorically pathetic, "To what am I to attribute this very unexpected pleasure, my dear Miss O'Carroll?"

MARIONETTA

I must apologize for intruding on you, Mr. Flosky; but the interest which I — you — take in my cousin Scythrop —

MR. FLOSKY

Pardon me, Miss O'Carroll; I do not take any interest in any person or thing on the face of the earth; which sentiment, if you analyze it, you will find to be the quintessence of the most refined philanthropy.

MARIONETTA

I will take it for granted that it is so, Mr. Flosky; I am not conversant with metaphysical subtleties, but —

MR. FLOSKY

Subtleties! my dear Miss O'Carroll. I am sorry to find you participating in the vulgar error of the reading public, to whom an unusual collocation of words, involving a juxtaposition of antiperistatical ideas, immediately suggests the notion of hyperoxysophistical paradoxology.

MARIONETTA

Indeed, Mr. Flosky, it suggests no such notion to me. I have sought you for the purpose of obtaining information.

MR. FLOSKY (*shaking his head*)

No one ever sought me for such a purpose before.

MARIONETTA

I think, Mr. Flosky — that is, I believe — that is, I fancy — that is, I imagine —

MR. FLOSKY

The *toutesti*, the *id est*, the *cioè*, the *c'est à dire*, the *that is*, my dear Miss O'Carroll, is not applicable in this case — if you will permit me to take the liberty of saying so. Think is not synonymous with believe — for belief, in many most important particulars, results from the total absence, the absolute negation of thought, and is thereby the sane and orthodox condition of mind; and thought and belief are both essentially different from fancy, and fancy, again, is distinct from imagination. This distinction between fancy and imagination is one of the most abstruse and important points of metaphysics. I have written seven hundred pages of promise to elucidate it, which promise I shall keep as faithfully as the bank will its promise to pay.

MARIONETTA

I assure you, Mr. Flosky, I care no more about metaphysics than I do about the bank; and, if you will condescend to talk to a simple girl in intelligible terms —

MR. FLOSKY

Say not condescend! Know you not that you talk to the most humble of men, to one who has buckled on the armor of sanctity, and clothed himself with humility as with a garment?

MARIONETTA

My cousin Scythrop has of late had an air of mystery about him, which gives me great uneasiness.

MR. FLOSKY

That is strange: nothing is so becoming to a man as an air of mystery. Mystery is the very keystone of all that is beautiful in poetry, all that is sacred in faith, and all that is recondite in transcendental psychology. I am writing a ballad which is all mystery; it is "such stuff as dreams are made of," and is, indeed, stuff made of a dream; for, last night I fell asleep as usual over my book, and had a vision of pure reason. I composed five hundred lines in my sleep; so that, having had a dream of a ballad, I am now officiating as my own Peter Quince, and making a ballad of my dream, and it shall be called Bottom's Dream, because it has no bottom.

MARIONETTA

I see, Mr. Flosky, you think my intrusion unseasonable, and are inclined to punish it, by talking nonsense to me. (*Mr. Flosky gave a start at the word nonsense, which almost overturned the table.*) I assure you, I would not have intruded if I had not been very much interested in the question I wish to ask you. — (*Mr. Flosky listened in sullen dignity.*) — My cousin Scythrop seems to have some secret preying on his mind. — (*Mr. Flosky was silent.*) — He seems very unhappy — Mr. Flosky — Perhaps you are acquainted with the cause. (*Mr. Flosky was still silent.*) — I only wish to know — Mr. Flosky — if it is any thing — that could be remedied by any thing that any one — of whom I know any thing — could do.

MR. FLOSKY

(*after a pause*)There are various ways of getting at secrets The most approved methods, as recommended both theoretically and practically in philosophical novels, are eavesdropping at keyholes, picking the locks of chests and desks, peeping into letters, steaming wafers, and insinuating hot wire under sealing wax; none of which methods I hold it lawful to practice.

MARIONETTA

Surely, Mr. Flosky, you cannot suspect me of wishing to adopt or encourage such base and contemptible arts.

MR. FLOSKY

Yet are they recommended, and with well-strung reasons, by writers of gravity and note, as simple and easy methods of studying character, and gratifying that laudable curiosity which aims at the knowledge of man.

MARIONETTA

I am as ignorant of this morality which you do not approve, as of the metaphysics which you do: I should be glad to know by your means, what is the matter with my cousin; I do not like to see him unhappy, and I suppose there is some reason for it.

MR. FLOSKY

Now I should rather suppose there is no reason for it: it is the fashion to be unhappy To have a reason for being so would be exceedingly commonplace: to be so without any is the province of genius: the art of being miserable for misery's sake, has been brought to great perfection in our days; and the ancient Odyssey, which held forth a shining example of the endurance of real misfortune, will give place to a modern one, setting out a more instructive picture of querulous impatience under imaginary evils.

MARIONETTA

Will you oblige me, Mr. Flosky, by giving me a plain answer to a plain question?

MR. FLOSKY

It is impossible, my dear Miss O'Carroll I never gave a plain answer to a question in my life.

MARIONETTA

Do you, or do you not, know what is the matter with my cousin?

MR. FLOSKY

To say that I do not know, would be to say that I am

ignorant of something; and God forbid, that a transcendental metaphysician, who has pure anticipated cognitions of everything, and carries the whole science of geometry in his head without ever having looked into Euclid, should fall into so empirical an error as to declare himself ignorant of any thing: to say that I do know, would be to pretend to positive and circumstantial knowledge touching present matter of fact, which, when you consider the nature of evidence, and the various lights in which the same thing may be seen —

MARIONETTA
I see, Mr. Flosky, that either you have no information, or are determined not to impart it; and I beg your pardon for having given you this unnecessary trouble.

MR. FLOSKY
My dear Miss O'Carroll, it would have given me great pleasure to have said any thing that would have given you pleasure; but if any person living could make report of having obtained any information on any subject from Ferdinando Flosky, my transcendental reputation would be ruined forever.

Chapter IX

Scythrop grew every day more reserved, mysterious, and distrait; and gradually lengthened the duration of his diurnal seclusions in his tower. Marionetta thought she perceived in all this very manifest symptoms of a warm love cooling.

It was seldom that she found herself alone with him in the morning, and, on these occasions, if she was silent in the hope of his speaking first, not a syllable would he utter; if she spoke to him indirectly, he assented monosyllabically; if she questioned him, his answers were brief, constrained, and evasive. Still, though her spirits were depressed, her playfulness had not so totally forsaken her, but that it illuminated at intervals the gloom of Nightmare Abbey; and if, on any occasion, she observed in Scythrop tokens of un-extinguished or returning passion, her love of torment-ing her lover immediately got the better both of her grief and her sympathy, though not of her curiosity, which Scythrop seemed determined not to satisfy. This playfulness, however, was in a great measure artificial, and usually vanished with the irritable Strephon, to whose annoyance it had been exerted. The Genius Loci, the tutela of Nightmare Abbey, the spirit of black melancholy, began to set his seal on her pallescent countenance. Scythrop perceived the change, found his tender sympathies awakened, and did his utmost to comfort the afflicted damsel, assuring her that his seeming inattention had only proceeded from his being involved in a profound meditation on a very hopeful scheme for the regeneration of human society. Marionetta called him ungrateful, cruel, cold-hearted, and accompanied her reproaches with many sobs and tears; poor Scythrop growing every moment more soft and submissive — till, at length, he threw himself at her feet, and declared that no competition of beauty, however dazzling, genius, however transcendent, talents, however cultivated, or philosophy, however enlightened, should ever make him renounce his divine Marionetta.

"Competition!" thought Marionetta, and suddenly, with an air of the most freezing indifference, she said, "You are perfectly at liberty, sir, to do as you please; I beg you will follow your own plans, without any reference to me."

Scythrop was confounded. What was become of all her passion and her tears? Still kneeling, he kissed her hand with rueful timidity, and said, in most pathetic accents, "Do you not love me, Marionetta?"

"No," said Marionetta, with a look of cold composure: "No." Scythrop still looked up incredulously. "No, I tell you."

"Oh! very well, madam," said Scythrop, rising, "if that is the case, there are those in the world —"

"To be sure there are, sir; — and do you suppose I do not see through your designs, you ungenerous monster?"

"My designs? Marionetta!"

"Yes, your designs, Scythrop. You have come here to

cast me off, and artfully contrive that it should appear to be my doing, and not yours, thinking to quiet your tender conscience with this pitiful stratagem. But do not suppose that you are of so much consequence to me: do not suppose it: you are of no consequence to me at all — none at all: therefore, leave me: I renounce you: leave me; why do you not leave me?"

Scythrop endeavored to remonstrate, but without success. She reiterated her injunctions to him to leave her, till, in the simplicity of his spirit, he was preparing to comply. When he had nearly reached the door, Marionetta said, "Farewell." Scythrop looked back. "Farewell, Scythrop," she repeated, "you will never see me again."

"Never see you again, Marionetta?"

"I shall go from hence tomorrow, perhaps today; and before we meet again, one of us will be married, and we might as well be dead, you know, Scythrop."

The sudden change of her voice in the last few words, and the burst of tears that accompanied them, acted like electricity on the tender-hearted youth; and, in another instant, a complete reconciliation was accomplished without the intervention of words.

There are, indeed, some learned casuists, who maintain that love has no language, and that all the misunderstandings and dissensions of lovers arise from the fatal habit of employing words on a subject to which words are inapplicable; that love, beginning with looks, that is to say, with the physiognomical expression of congenial mental dispositions, tends through a regular gradation of signs and symbols of affection, to that consummation which is most devoutly to be wished; and that it neither is necessary that there should be, nor probable that there would be, a single word spoken from first to last between two sympathetic spirits, were it not that the arbitrary institutions of society have raised, at every step of this very simple process, so many complicated impediments and barriers in the shape of settlements and ceremonies, parents and guardians, lawyers, Jew-brokers, and parsons, that many an adventurous knight (who, in order to obtain the conquest of the Hesperian fruit, is obliged to fight his way through all these monsters), is either repulsed at the onset, or vanquished before the achievement of his enterprise: and such a quantity of unnatural talking is rendered inevitably necessary through all the stages of the progression, that the tender and volatile spirit of love often takes flight on the pinions of some of the *epea pteroenta*, or winged words which are pressed into his service in despite of himself.

At this conjuncture, Mr. Glowry entered, and sitting down near them, said, "I see how it is; and, as we are all sure to be miserable do what we may, there is no need of taking pains to make one another more so; therefore, with God's blessing and mine, there" — joining their hands as he spoke.

Scythrop was not exactly prepared for this decisive step; but he could only stammer out, "Really, sir, you are too good;" and Mr. Glowry departed to bring Mr. Hilary to ratify the act.

Now, whatever truth there may be in the theory of love and language, of which we have so recently spoken, certain it is, that during Mr. Glowry's absence, which lasted half an hour, not a single word was said by either Scythrop or Marionetta.

Mr. Glowry returned with Mr. Hilary, who was delighted at the prospect of so advantageous an establishment for his orphan niece, of whom he considered himself in some manner the guardian, and nothing remained, as Mr. Glowry observed, but to fix the day.

Marionetta blushed, and was silent. Scythrop was also silent for a time, and at length hesitatingly said,

"My dear sir, your goodness overpowers me; but really you are so precipitate."

Now, this remark, if the young lady had made it, would, whether she thought it or not — for sincerity is a thing of no account on these occasions, nor indeed on any other, according to Mr. Flosky — this remark, if the young lady had made it, would have been perfectly *comme il faut*; but, being made by the young gentleman, it was *toute autre chose*, and was, indeed, in the eyes of his mistress, a most heinous and irremissible offence. Marionetta was angry, very angry, but she concealed her anger, and said, calmly and coldly, "Certainly, you are much too precipitate, Mr. Glowry. I assure you, sir, I have by no means made up my mind; and, indeed, as far as I know it, it inclines the other way; but it will be quite time enough to think of these matters seven years hence." Before surprise permitted reply, the young lady had locked herself up in her own apartment.

"Why, Scythrop," said Mr. Glowry, elongating his face exceedingly, "the devil is come among us sure enough, as Mr. Toobad observes: I thought you and Marionetta were both of a mind."

"So we are, I believe, sir," said Scythrop, gloomily, and stalked away to his tower.

"Mr. Glowry," said Mr. Hilary, "I do not very well understand all this."

"Whims, brother Hilary," said Mr. Glowry; "some little foolish love quarrel, nothing more. Whims, freaks, April showers. They will be blown over by tomorrow."

"If not," said Mr. Hilary, "these April showers have made us April fools."

"Ah!" said Mr. Glowry, "you are a happy man, and in all your afflictions you can console yourself with a joke, let it be ever so bad, provided you crack it yourself. I should be very happy to laugh with you, if it would give you any satisfaction; but, really, at present, my heart is so sad, that I find it impossible to levy a contribution on my muscles."

Chapter X

On the evening on which Mr. Asterias had caught a glimpse of a female figure on the seashore, which he had translated into the visual sign of his interior cognition of a mermaid, Scythrop, retiring to his tower, found his study preoccupied. A stranger, muffled in a cloak, was sitting at his table. Scythrop paused in surprise. The stranger rose at his entrance, and looked at him intently a few minutes, in silence. The eyes of the stranger alone were visible. All the rest of the figure was muffled and mantled in the folds of a black cloak, which was raised, by the right hand, to the level of the eyes. This scrutiny being completed, the stranger, dropping the cloak, said, "I see, by your physiognomy, that you may be trusted;" and revealed to the astonished Scythrop a female form and countenance of dazzling grace and beauty, with long flowing hair of raven blackness, and large black eyes of almost oppressive brilliancy, which strikingly contrasted with a complexion of snowy whiteness. Her dress was extremely elegant, but had an appearance of foreign fashion, as if both the lady and her mantua-maker were of "a far countree."

"I guess 'twas frightful there to see
A lady so richly clad as she,
Beautiful exceedingly."

For, if it be terrible to one young lady to find another
under a tree at midnight, it must, *a fortiori,* be much
more terrible to a young gentleman to find a young
lady in his study at that hour. If the logical consecu-
tiveness of this conclusion be not manifest to my
readers, I am sorry for their dullness, and must refer
them, for more ample elucidation, to a treatise which
Mr. Flosky intends to write, on the Categories of Relation, which comprehend Substance and Accident,
Cause and Effect, Action and Reaction.

Scythrop, therefore, either was or ought to have been
frightened; at all events, he was astonished; and
astonishment, though not in itself fear, is nevertheless
a good stage towards it, and is, indeed, as it were, the
half-way house between respect and terror, according
to Mr. Burke's graduated scale of the sublime.*

---

* There must be some mistake in this, for the whole honorable band of gentlemen-pensioners has resolved unani-
mously, that Mr. Burke was a very sublime person,
particularly after he had prostituted his own soul, and be-
trayed his country and mankind, for 1200*l.* a year: yet he
does not appear to have been a very terrible personage,
and certainly went off with a very small portion of human
respect, though he contrived to excite, in a great degree,
the astonishment of all honest men. Our immaculate laure-
ate [Southey] (who gives us to understand that, if he had
not been purified by holy matrimony into a mystical type,
he would have died a virgin,) is another sublime gentleman of the same genus: he very much astonished some persons when he sold his birthright for a pot of sack; but not
even his Sosia has a grain of respect for him, though,
doubtless, he thinks his name very terrible to the enemy,
when he flourishes his criticopoeticopolitical tomahawk,
and sets up his Indian yell for the blood of his old friends:

"You are surprised," said the lady; "yet why should you be surprised? If you had met me in a drawing room, and I had been introduced to you by an old woman, it would have been a matter of course: can the division of two or three walls, and the absence of an unimportant personage, make the same object essentially different in the perception of a philosopher?"

"Certainly not," said Scythrop; "but when any class of objects has habitually presented itself to our perceptions in invariable conjunction with particular relations, then, on the sudden appearance of one object of the class divested of those accompaniments, the essential difference of the relation is, by an involuntary process, transferred to the object itself, which thus offers itself to our perceptions with all the strangeness of novelty."

"You are a philosopher," said the lady, "and a lover of liberty. You are the author of a treatise, called 'Philosophical Gas; or, a Project for a General Illumination of the Human Mind.'"

"I am," said Scythrop, delighted at this first blossom of his renown.

"I am a stranger in this country," said the lady; "I have been but a few days in it, yet I find myself immediately under the necessity of seeking refuge from an atrocious persecution. I had no friend to whom I could apply; and, in the midst of my difficulties, accident threw your pamphlet in my way. I saw that I had, at least, one kindred mind in this nation, and determined to apply to you."

"And what would you have me do?" said Scythrop, more and more amazed, and not a little perplexed.

---

but, at best, he is a mere political scarecrow, a man of straw, ridiculous to all who know of what material he is made; and to none more so, than to those who have stuffed him, and set him up, as the Priapus of the garden of the golden apples of corruption.

"I would have you," said the young lady, "assist me in finding some place of retreat, where I can remain concealed from the indefatigable search that is being made for me. I have been so nearly caught once or twice already, that I cannot confide any longer in my own ingenuity."

Doubtless, thought Scythrop, this is one of my golden candlesticks. "I have constructed," said he, "in this tower, an entrance to a small suite of unknown apartments in the main building, which I defy any creature living to detect. If you would like to remain there a day or two, till I can find you a more suitable concealment, you may rely on the honor of a transcendental eleutherarch."

"I rely on myself," said the lady. "I act as I please, go where I please, and let the world say what it will. I am rich enough to set it at defiance. It is the tyrant of the poor and the feeble, but the slave of those who are above the reach of its injury."

Scythrop ventured to inquire the name of his fair *protégée*. "What is a name?" said the lady: "any name will serve the purpose of distinction. Call me Stella. I see by your looks," she added, "that you think all this very strange. When you know me better, your surprise will cease. I submit not to be an accomplice in my sex's slavery. I am, like yourself, a lover of freedom, and I carry my theory into practice. *They alone are subject to blind authority who have no reliance on their own strength.*"

Stella took possession of the recondite apartments. Scythrop intended to find her another asylum; but from day to day he postponed his intention, and by degrees forgot it. The young lady reminded him of it from day to day, till she also forgot it. Scythrop was anxious to learn her history; but she would add nothing to what she had already communicated, that she was shunning an atrocious persecution. Scythrop thought of Lord C. and the Alien Act, and said, "As you will not tell your name, I suppose it is in the green bag." Stella, not understanding what he meant, was silent; and Scythrop, translating silence into acquiescence, concluded that he was sheltering an *illuminee* whom Lord S. suspected of an intention to take the Tower, and set fire to the Bank: exploits, at least, as likely to be accomplished by the hands and eyes of a young beauty, as by a drunken cobbler and doctor, armed with a pamphlet and an old stocking.

Stella, in her conversations with Scythrop, displayed a highly cultivated and energetic mind, full of impassioned schemes of liberty, and impatience of masculine usurpation. She had a lively sense of all the oppressions that are done under the sun; and the vivid pictures which her imagination presented to her of the numberless scenes of injustice and misery which are being acted at every moment in every part of the inhabited world, gave an habitual seriousness to her physiognomy, that made it seem as if a smile had never once hovered on her lips. She was intimately conversant with the German language and literature; and Scythrop listened with delight to her repetitions of her favorite passages from Schiller and Goethe, and to her encomiums on the sublime Spartacus Weishaupt, the immortal founder of the sect of the Illuminati. Scythrop found that his soul had a greater capacity of love than the image of Marionetta had filled. The form of Stella took possession of every vacant corner of the cavity, and by degrees displaced that of Marionetta from many of the outworks of the citadel; though the latter still held possession of the keep. He judged, from his new friend calling herself Stella, that, if it were not her real name, she was an admirer of the principles of the German play from which she had taken it, and took an opportunity of leading the conversation to that subject; but to his great surprise, the lady spoke very ardently of the singleness and exclusiveness of love, and declared that the reign of affection was one and indivisible; that it might be transferred, but could not be participated. "If I ever love," said she, "I shall do so without limit or restriction. I shall hold all difficulties light, all sacrifices cheap, all obstacles gossamer. But for love so total, I shall claim a return as absolute. I will have no rival: whether more or less favored will be of little moment. I will be neither first nor second — I will be alone. The heart which I shall possess I will possess entirely, or entirely renounce."

Scythrop did not dare to mention the name of Marionetta; he trembled lest some unlucky accident should reveal it to Stella, though he scarcely knew what result to wish or anticipate, and lived in the double fever of a perpetual dilemma. He could not dissemble to himself that he was in love, at the same time, with two damsels of minds and habits as remote as the antipodes. The scale of predilection always inclined to the fair one who happened to be present; but the absent was never effectually outweighed, though the degrees of exaltation and depression varied according to accidental variations in the outward and visible signs of the inward and spiritual graces of his respective charmers. Passing and repassing several times a day from the company of the one to that of the other, he was like a shuttlecock between two battledores, changing its direction as rapidly as the oscillations of a pendulum, receiving many a hard knock on the cork of a sensitive heart, and flying from point to point on the feathers of a super-sublimated head. This was an awful state of things. He had now as much mystery about him as any romantic transcendentalist or transcendental romancer could desire. He had his esoterical and his exoterical love. He could not endure the thought of losing either of them, but he trembled when he imagined the possibility that some fatal discovery might deprive him of both. The old proverb concerning two strings to a bow gave him some gleams of comfort; but that concerning two stools occurred to him more frequently, and covered his forehead with a cold perspiration. With Stella, he could indulge freely in all his romantic and philosophical visions. He could build castles in the air, and she would pile towers and turrets on the imaginary edifices. With Marionetta it was otherwise: she knew nothing of the world and society beyond the sphere of her own experience. Her life was all music and sunshine, and she wondered what any one could see to complain of in such a pleasant state of things. She loved Scythrop, she hardly knew why; indeed she was not always sure that she loved him at all: she felt her fondness increase or diminish in an inverse ratio to his. When she had maneuvered him into a fever of passionate love, she often felt and always assumed indifference: if she found that her coldness was contagious, and that Scythrop either was, or pretended to be, as indifferent as herself, she would become doubly kind, and raise him again to that elevation from which she had previously thrown him down. Thus, when his love was flowing, hers was ebbing: when his was ebbing, hers was flowing. Now and then there were moments of level tide, when reciprocal affection seemed to promise imperturbable harmony; but Scythrop could scarcely resign his spirit to the pleasing illusion, before the pinnace of the lover's affections was caught in some eddy of the lady's caprice, and he was whirled away from the shore of his hopes, without rudder or compass, into an ocean of mists and storms. It resulted, from this system of conduct, that all that passed between Scythrop and Marionetta consisted in making and unmaking love. He had no opportunity to take measure of her understanding by conversations on general subjects, and on his favorite designs; and, being left in this respect to the exercise of indefinite conjecture, he took it for granted, as most lovers would do in similar circumstances, that she had great natural talents, which she wasted at present on trifles: but coquetry would end with marriage, and leave room for philosophy to exert its influence on her mind. Stella had no coquetry, no disguise: she was an enthusiast in subjects of general interest; and her conduct to Scythrop was always uniform, or rather showed a regular progression of partiality which seemed fast ripening into love.

Chapter XI

Scythrop, attending one day the summons to dinner, found in the drawing room his friend Mr. Cypress the poet, whom he had known at college, and who was a great favorite of Mr. Glowry. Mr. Cypress said, he was on the point of leaving England, but could not think of doing so without a farewell-look at Nightmare Abbey and his respected friends, the moody Mr. Glowry and the mysterious Mr. Scythrop, the sublime Mr. Flosky and the pathetic Mr. Listless; to all of whom, and the morbid hospitality of the melancholy dwelling in which they were then assembled, he assured them he should always look back with as much affection as his lacerated spirit could feel for any thing. The sympathetic condolence of their respective replies was cut short by Raven's announcement of "dinner on table."

The conversation that took place when the wine was in circulation, and the ladies were withdrawn, we shall report with our usual scrupulous fidelity.

MR. GLOWRY
You are leaving England, Mr. Cypress. There is a delightful melancholy in saying farewell to an old

acquaintance, when the chances are twenty to one
against ever meeting again. A smiling bumper to a sad
parting, and let us all be unhappy together.

MR. CYPRESS (*filling a bumper*)
This is the only social habit that the disappointed
spirit never unlearns.

THE REVEREND MR. LARYNX (*filling*)
It is the only piece of academical learning that the
finished educatee retains.

MR. FLOSKY (*filling*)
It is the only objective fact which the skeptic can
realize.

SCYTHROP (*filling*)
It is the only styptic for a bleeding heart.

THE HONORABLE MR. LISTLESS (*filling*)
It is the only trouble that is very well worth taking.

MR. ASTERIAS (*filling*)
It is the only key of conversational truth.
MR. TOOBAD (*filling*)
It is the only antidote to the great wrath of the devil.
MR. HILARY (*filling*)
It is the only symbol of perfect life. The inscription
"HIC NON BIBITUR" will suit nothing but a tomb-
stone.

MR. GLOWRY
You will see many fine old ruins, Mr. Cypress; crum-
bling pillars, and mossy walls — many a one-legged
Venus and headless Minerva — many a Neptune buried
in sand — many a Jupiter turned topsy-turvy — many

a perforated Bacchus doing duty as a water pipe —
many reminiscences of the ancient world, which I hope
was better worth living in than the modern; though,
for myself, I care not a straw more for one than the
other, and would not go twenty miles to see any thing
that either could show.

MR. CYPRESS

It is something to seek, Mr. Glowry. The mind is
restless, and must persist in seeking, though to find is
to be disappointed. Do you feel no aspirations towards
the countries of Socrates and Cicero? No wish to
wander among the venerable remains of the greatness
that has passed forever?

MR. GLOWRY

Not a grain.

SCYTHROP

It is, indeed, much the same as if a lover should dig
up the buried form of his mistress, and gaze upon relics
which are any thing but herself, to wander among a
few moldy ruins, that are only imperfect indexes to lost
volumes of glory, and meet at every step the more
melancholy ruins of human nature — a degenerate race
of stupid and shriveled slaves, groveling in the lowest
depths of servility and superstition.

THE HONORABLE MR. LISTLESS

It is the fashion to go abroad. I have thought of it
myself, but am hardly equal to the exertion. To be sure,
a little eccentricity and originality are allowable in
some cases; and the most eccentric and original of all
characters is an Englishman who stays at home.

SCYTHROP

I should have no pleasure in visiting countries that are past all hope of regeneration. There is great hope of our own; and it seems to me that an Englishman, who, either by his station in society, or by his genius, or (as in your instance, Mr. Cypress,) by both, has the power of essentially serving his country in its arduous struggle with its domestic enemies, yet forsakes his country, which is still so rich in hope, to dwell in others which are only fertile in the ruins of memory, does what none of those ancients, whose fragmentary memorials you venerate, would have done in similar circumstances.

MR. CYPRESS

Sir, I have quarreled with my wife; and a man who has quarreled with his wife is absolved from all duty to his country. I have written an ode to tell the people as much, and they may take it as they list.

SCYTHROP

Do you suppose, if Brutus had quarreled with his wife, he would have given it as a reason to Cassius for having nothing to do with his enterprise? Or would Cassius have been satisfied with such an excuse?

MR. FLOSKY

Brutus was a senator; so is our dear friend: but the cases are different. Brutus had some hope of political good: Mr. Cypress has none. How should he, after what we have seen in France?

SCYTHROP

A Frenchman is born in harness, ready saddled, bitted, and bridled, for any tyrant to ride. He will fawn under his rider one moment, and throw him and kick him to death the next; but another adventurer springs on his back, and by dint of whip and spur on he goes as before. We may, without much vanity, hope better of ourselves.

MR. CYPRESS

I have no hope for myself or for others. Our life is a false nature; it is not in the harmony of things; it is an all-blasting upas, whose root is earth, and whose leaves are the skies which rain their poison-dews upon mankind. We wither from our youth; we gasp with unslaked thirst for unattainable good; lured from the first to the last by phantoms — love, fame, ambition, avarice — all idle, and all ill — one meteor of many names, that vanishes in the smoke of death.

MR. FLOSKY

A most delightful speech, Mr. Cypress. A most amiable and instructive philosophy. You have only to impress its truth on the minds of all living men, and life will then, indeed, be the desert and the solitude; and I must do you, myself, and our mutual friends, the justice to observe, that let society only give fair play at one and the same time, as I flatter myself it is inclined to do, to your system of morals, and my system of metaphysics, and Scythrop's system of politics, and Mr. Listless's system of manners, and Mr. Toobad's system of religion, and the result will be as fine a mental chaos as even the immortal Kant himself could ever have hoped to see; in the prospect of which I rejoice.

MR. HILARY

"Certainly, ancient, it is not a thing to rejoice at:" I am one of those who cannot see the good that is to result from all this mystifying and blue-devilling of

society. The contrast it presents to the cheerful and
solid wisdom of antiquity is too forcible not to strike
any one who has the least knowledge of classical literature. To represent vice and misery as the necessary
accompaniments of genius, is as mischievous as it is
false, and the feeling is as unclassical as the language
in which it is usually expressed.

MR. TOOBAD

It is our calamity. The devil has come among us, and
has begun by taking possession of all the cleverest
fellows. Yet, forsooth, this is the enlightened age.
Marry, how? Did our ancestors go peeping about with
dark lanterns, and do we walk at our ease in broad
sunshine? Where is the manifestation of our light? By
what symptoms do you recognize it? What are its signs,
its tokens, its symptoms, its symbols, its categories, its
conditions? What is it, and why? How, where, when is
it to be seen, felt, and understood? What do we see by
it which our ancestors saw not, and which at the same
time is worth seeing? We see a hundred men hanged,
where they saw one. We see five hundred transported,
where they saw one. We see five thousand in the work-
house, when they saw one. We see scores of Bible
Societies, where they saw none. We see paper, where
they saw gold. We see men in stays, where they saw men
in armor. We see painted faces, where they saw healthy
ones. We see children perishing in manufactories,
where they saw them flourishing in the fields. We see
prisons, where they saw castles. We see masters, where
they saw representatives. In short, they saw true men,
where we see false knaves. They saw Milton, and we see
Mr. Sackbut.

MR. FLOSKY

The false knave, sir, is my honest friend; therefore,

1 beseech you, let him be countenanced. God forbid but a knave should have some countenance at his friend's request.

MR. TOOBAD

"Good men and true" was their common term, like the kalos kagathos of the Athenians. It is so long since men have been either good or true, that it is to be questioned which is most obsolete, the fact or the phraseology.

MR. CYPRESS

There is no worth nor beauty but in the mind's idea. Love sows the wind and reaps the whirlwind. Confusion, thrice confounded, is the portion of him who rests even for an instant on that most brittle of reeds — the affection of a human being. The sum of our social destiny is to inflict or to endure.

MR. HILARY

Rather to bear and forbear, Mr. Cypress — a maxim which you perhaps despise. Ideal beauty is not the mind's creation: it is real beauty, refined and purified in the mind's alembic, from the alloy which always more or less accompanies it in our mixed and imperfect nature. But still the gold exists in a very ample degree. To expect too much is a disease in the expectant, for which human nature is not responsible; and, in the common name of humanity, I protest against these false and mischievous ravings. To rail against humanity for not being abstract perfection, and against human love for not realizing all the splendid visions of the poets of chivalry, is to rail at the summer for not being all sunshine, and at the rose for not being always in bloom.

MR. CYPRESS

Human love! Love is not an inhabitant of the earth. We worship him as the Athenians did their unknown God: but broken hearts are the martyrs of his faith, and the eye shall never see the form which phantasy paints, and which passion pursues through paths of delusive beauty, among flowers whose odors are agonies, and trees whose gums are poison.

MR. HILARY

You talk like a Rosicrucian, who will love nothing but a sylph, who does not believe in the existence of a sylph, and who yet quarrels with the whole universe for not containing a sylph.

MR. CYPRESS

The mind is diseased of its own beauty, and fevers into false creation. The forms which the sculptor's soul has seized exist only in himself.

MR. FLOSKY

Permit me to discept. They are the mediums of common forms combined and arranged into a common standard. The ideal beauty of the Helen of Zeuxis was the combined medium of the real beauty of the virgins of Crotona.

MR. HILARY

But to make ideal beauty the shadow in the water, and, like the dog in the fable, to throw away the substance in catching at the shadow, is scarcely the characteristic of wisdom, whatever it may be of genius. To reconcile man as he is to the world as it is, to preserve and improve all that is good, and destroy or alleviate all that is evil, in physical and moral nature — have been the hope and aim of the greatest teachers and ornaments of our species. I will say, too, that the highest wisdom and the highest genius have been invariably accompanied with cheerfulness. We have sufficient proofs on record that Shakespeare and Socrates were the most festive of companions. But now the little wisdom and genius we have seem to be entering into a conspiracy against cheerfulness.

MR. TOOBAD
How can we be cheerful with the devil among us?

THE HONORABLE MR. LISTLESS
How can we be cheerful when our nerves are shattered?

MR. FLOSKY
How can we be cheerful when we are surrounded by a reading public, that is growing too wise for its betters?

SCYTHROP
How can we be cheerful when our great general designs are crossed every moment by our little particular passions?

MR. CYPRESS
How can we be cheerful in the midst of disappointment and despair?

MR. GLOWRY
Let us all be unhappy together.

MR. HILARY
Let us sing a catch.

MR. GLOWRY
No: a nice tragical ballad. The Norfolk Tragedy to

the tune of the Hundredth Psalm.

MR. HILARY

I say a catch.

MR. GLOWRY

I say no. A song from Mr. Cypress.

ALL

A song from Mr. Cypress.

MR. CYPRESS *sung* —

There is a fever of the spirit,
   The brand of Cain's unresting doom,
Which in the lone dark souls that bear it
   Glows like the lamp in Tullia's tomb:
Unlike that lamp, its subtle fire
   Burns, blasts, consumes its cell, the heart,
Till, one by one, hope, joy, desire,
   Like dreams of shadowy smoke depart.
When hope, love, life itself, are only
   Dust — spectral memories — dead and cold —
The unfed fire burns bright and lonely,
   Like that undying lamp of old:
And by that drear illumination,
   Till time its clay-built home has rent,
Thought broods on feeling's desolation —
   The soul is its own monument.

MR. GLOWRY

Admirable. Let us all be unhappy together.

MR. HILARY

Now, I say again, a catch.

THE REVEREND MR. LARYNX

I am for you.

MR. HILARY

"Seamen three."

THE REVEREND MR. LARYNX

Agreed. I'll be Harry Gill, with the voice of three.
Begin.

MR. HILARY AND
THE REVEREND MR. LARYNX

Seamen three! What men be ye?
Gotham's three wise men we be.
Whither in your bowl so free?
To rake the moon from out the sea.
The bowl goes trim. The moon doth shine.
And our ballast is oldwine;
And your ballast is old wine.
Who art thou, so fast adrift?
I am he they call Old Care.
Here on board we will thee lift.
No: I may not enter there.
Wherefore so? 'Tis Jove's decree,
In a bowl Care may not be;
In a bowl Care may not be.
Fear ye not the waves that roll?
No: in charmed bowl we swim.
What the charm that floats the bowl?
Water may not pass the brim.
The bowl goes trim. The moon doth shine.
And our ballast is old wine;
And your ballast is old wine.

This catch was so well executed by the spirit and
science of Mr. Hilary, and the deep tri-une voice of the
reverend gentleman, that the whole party, in spite of
themselves, caught the contagion, and joined in chorus
at the conclusion, each raising a bumper to his lips:

The bowl goes trim: the moon doth shine:
And our ballast is old wine.

Mr. Cypress, having his ballast on board, stepped, the same evening, into his bowl, or traveling chariot, and departed to rake seas and rivers, lakes and canals, for the moon of ideal beauty.

Chapter XII

*I*t was the custom of the Honorable Mr. Listless, on adjourning from the bottle to the ladies, to retire for a few moments to make a second toilette, that he might present himself in becoming taste. Fatout, attending as usual, appeared with a countenance of great dismay, and informed his master that he had just ascertained that the abbey was haunted. Mr. Hilary's *gentlewoman,* for whom Fatout had lately conceived a *tendresse,* had been, as she expressed it, "fritted out of her seventeen senses" the preceding night, as she was retiring to her bedchamber, by a ghastly figure which she had met stalking along one of the galleries, wrapped in a white shroud, with a bloody turban on its head. She had fainted away with fear; and, when she recovered, she found herself in the dark, and the figure was gone. *"Sacre — cochon — bleu!"* exclaimed Fatout, giving very deliberate emphasis to every portion of his terrible oath "I vould not meet de *revenant,* de ghost — *non* — not for all de *bowl-de-ponch* in de vorld."

"Fatout," said the Honorable Mr. Listless, "did I ever see a ghost?"

"Jamais, monsieur, never."

"Then I hope I never shall, for, in the present shattered state of my nerves, I am afraid it would be too
much for me. There — loosen the lace of my stays a
little, for really this plebeian practice of eating — Not
too loose — consider my shape. That will do. And I
desire that you bring me no more stories of ghosts; for,
though I do not believe in such things, yet, when one
is awake in the night, one is apt, if one thinks of them,
to have fancies that give one a kind of a chill, particularly if one opens one's eyes suddenly on one's dressing
gown, hanging in the moonlight, between the bed and
the window."

The Honorable Mr. Listless, though he had prohib-
ited Fatout from bringing him any more stories of
ghosts, could not help thinking of that which Fatout
had already brought; and, as it was uppermost in his
mind, when he descended to the tea and coffee cups,
and the rest of the company in the library, he almost
involuntarily asked Mr. Flosky, whom he looked up
to as a most oraculous personage, whether any story
of any ghost that had ever appeared to any one, was
entitled to any degree of belief?

MR. FLOSKY

By far the greater number, to a very great degree.

THE HONORABLE MR. LISTLESS

Really, that is very alarming!

MR. FLOSKY

Sunt geminæ somni portæ. There are two gates through
which ghosts find their way to the upper air: fraud and
self-delusion. In the latter case, a ghost is a deceptio
vis s, an ocular spectrum, an idea with the force of a
sensation. I have seen many ghosts myself. I dare say
there are few in this company who have not seen a

ghost.

THE HONORABLE MR. LISTLESS
I am happy to say, I never have, for one.

THE REVEREND MR. LARYNX
We have such high authority for ghosts, that it is rank skepticism to disbelieve them. Job saw a ghost, which came for the express purpose of asking a question, and did not wait for an answer.

THE HONORABLE MR. LISTLESS
Because Job was too frightened to give one.

THE REVEREND MR. LARYNX
Specters appeared to the Egyptians during the darkness with which Moses covered Egypt. The witch of Endor raised the ghost of Samuel. Moses and Elias appeared on Mount Tabor. An evil spirit was sent into the army of Sennacherib, and exterminated it in a single night.

MR. TOOBAD
Saying, The devil is come among you, having great wrath.

MR. FLOSKY
Saint Macarius interrogated a skull, which was found in the desert, and made it relate, in presence of several witnesses, what was going forward in hell. Saint Martin of Tours, being jealous of a pretended martyr, who was the rival saint of his neighborhood, called up his ghost, and made him confess that he was damned. Saint Germain, being on his travels, turned out of an inn a large party of ghosts, who had every night taken possession of the table d'hôte, and consumed a copious

supper.

MR. HILARY
Jolly ghosts, and no doubt all friars. A similar party took possession of the cellar of M. Swebach, the painter, in Paris, drank his wine, and threw the empty bottles at his head.

THE REVEREND MR. LARYNX
An atrocious act.

MR. FLOSKY
Pausanias relates, that the neighing of horses and the tumult of combatants were heard every night on the field of Marathon: that those who went purposely to hear these sounds suffered severely for their curiosity; but those who heard them by accident passed with impunity.

THE REVEREND MR. LARYNX
I once saw a ghost myself, in my study, which is the last place where any one but a ghost would look for me. I had not been into it for three months, and was going to consult Tillotson, when, on opening the door, I saw a venerable figure in a flannel dressing gown, sitting in my armchair, and reading my Jeremy Taylor. It vanished in a moment, and so did I; and what it was or what it wanted I have never been able to ascertain.

MR. FLOSKY
It was an idea with the force of a sensation. It is seldom that ghosts appeal to two senses at once; but, when I was in Devonshire, the following story was well attested to me. A young woman, whose lover was at sea, returning one evening over some solitary fields, saw her lover sitting on a stile over which she was to

pass. Her first emotions were surprise and joy, but there was a paleness and seriousness in his face that made them give place to alarm. She advanced towards him, and he said to her, in a solemn voice, "The eye that hath seen me shall see me no more. Thine eye is upon me, but I am not." And with these words he vanished; and on that very day and hour, as it afterwards appeared, he had perished by shipwreck.

The whole party now drew round in a circle, and each related some ghostly anecdote, heedless of the flight of time, till, in a pause of the conversation, they heard the hollow tongue of midnight sounding twelve.

MR. HILARY

All these anecdotes admit of solution on psychological principles. It is more easy for a soldier, a philosopher, or even a saint, to be frightened at his own shadow, than for a dead man to come out of his grave. Medical writers cite a thousand singular examples of the force of imagination. Persons of feeble, nervous, melancholy temperament, exhausted by fever, by labor, or by spare diet, will readily conjure up, in the magic ring of their own phantasy, specters, gorgons, chimæras, and all the objects of their hatred and their love. We are most of us like Don Quixote, to whom a windmill was a giant, and Dulcinea a magnificent princess: all more or less the dupes of our own imagination, though we do not all go so far as to see ghosts, or to fancy ourselves pipkins and teapots.

MR. FLOSKY

I can safely say I have seen too many ghosts myself to believe in their external existence. I have seen all kinds of ghosts: black spirits and white, red spirits and grey. Some in the shapes of venerable old men, who have met me in my rambles at noon; some of beautiful young women, who have peeped through my curtains at midnight.

THE HONORABLE MR. LISTLESS

And have proved, I doubt not, "palpable to feeling as to sight."

MR. FLOSKY

By no means, sir. You reflect upon my purity. Myself and my friends, particularly my friend Mr. Sackbut, are famous for our purity. No, sir, genuine untangible ghosts. I live in a world of ghosts. I see a ghost at this moment.

Mr. Flosky fixed his eyes on a door at the farther end of the library. The company looked in the same direction. The door silently opened, and a ghastly figure, shrouded in white drapery, with the semblance of a bloody turban on its head, entered and stalked slowly up the apartment. Mr. Flosky, familiar as he was with ghosts, was not prepared for this apparition, and made the best of his way out at the opposite door. Mrs. Hilary and Marionetta followed, screaming. The Honorable Mr. Listless, by two turns of his body, rolled first off the sofa and then under it. The Reverend Mr. Larynx leaped up and fled with so much precipitation, that he overturned the table on the foot of Mr. Glowry. Mr. Glowry roared with pain in the ear of Mr. Toobad. Mr. Toobad's alarm so bewildered his senses, that, missing the door, he threw up one of the windows, jumped out in his panic, and plunged over head and ears in the moat. Mr. Asterias and his son, who were on the watch for their mermaid, were attracted by the splashing, threw a net over him, and dragged him to land.

Scythrop and Mr. Hilary meanwhile had hastened to his assistance, and, on arriving at the edge of the moat, followed by several servants with ropes and torches, found Mr. Asterias and Aquarius busy in endeavoring to extricate Mr. Toobad from the net, who was entangled in the meshes, and floundering with rage. Scythrop was lost in amazement; but Mr. Hilary saw, at one view, all the circumstances of the adventure, and burst into an immoderate fit of laughter; on recovering from which, he said to Mr. Asterias, "You have caught an odd fish, indeed." Mr. Toobad was highly exasperated at this unseasonable pleasantry; but Mr. Hilary softened his anger, by producing a knife, and cutting the Gordian knot of his reticular envelopment. "You see," said Mr. Toobad, "you see, gentlemen, in my unfortunate person proof upon proof of the present dominion of the devil in the affairs of this world; and I have no doubt but that the apparition of this night was Apollyon himself in disguise, sent for the express purpose of terrifying me into this complication of misadventures. The devil is come among you, having great wrath, because he knoweth that he hath but a short time."

Chapter XIII

Mr. Glowry was much surprised, on occasionally visiting Scythrop's tower, to find the door always locked, and to be kept sometimes waiting many minutes for admission: during which he invariably heard a heavy rolling sound like that of a ponderous mangle, or of a wagon on a weighing bridge, or of theatrical thunder.

He took little notice of this for some time; at length his curiosity was excited, and, one day, instead of knocking at the door, as usual, the instant he reached it, he applied his ear to the keyhole, and like Bottom, in the Midsummer Night's Dream, "spied a voice," which he guessed to be of the feminine gender, and knew to be not Scythrop's, whose deeper tones he distinguished at intervals. Having attempted in vain to catch a syllable of the discourse, he knocked violently at the door, and roared for immediate admission. The voices ceased, the accustomed rolling sound was heard, the door opened, and Scythrop was discovered alone. Mr. Glowry looked round to every corner of the apartment, and then said, "Where is the lady?"

"The lady, sir?" said Scythrop.

"Yes, sir, the lady."

"Sir, I do not understand you."

"You don't, sir?"

"No, indeed, sir. There is no lady here."

"But, sir, this is not the only apartment in the tower, and I make no doubt there is a lady up stairs."

"You are welcome to search, sir."

"Yes, and while I am searching, she will slip out from some lurking place, and make her escape."

"You may lock this door, sir, and take the key with you."

"But there is the terrace door: she has escaped by the terrace."

"The terrace, sir, has no other outlet, and the walls are too high for a lady to jump down."

"Well, sir, give me the key."

Mr. Glowry took the key, searched every nook of the tower, and returned.

"You are a fox, Scythrop, you are an exceedingly cunning fox, with that demure visage of yours. What was that lumbering sound I heard before you opened the door?"

"Sound, sir?"

"Yes, sir, sound."

"My dear sir, I am not aware of any sound, except my great table, which I moved on rising to let you in."

"The table! — let me see that. No, sir; not a tenth part heavy enough, not a tenth part."

"But, sir, you do not consider the laws of acoustics: a whisper becomes a peal of thunder in the focus of reverberation. Allow me to explain this: sounds striking on concave surfaces are reflected from them, and, after reflection, converge to points which are the foci of these surfaces. It follows, therefore, that the ear may be so placed in one, that it shall hear a sound better than when situated nearer to the point of the first impulse: again, in the case of two concave surfaces placed opposite to each other —"

"Nonsense, sir. Don't tell me of foci. Pray, sir, will concave surfaces produce two voices when nobody speaks? I heard two voices, and one was feminine; feminine, sir: what say you to that?"

"Oh, sir, I perceive your mistake: I am writing a tragedy, and was acting over a scene to myself. To convince you, I will give you a specimen; but you must first understand the plot. It is a tragedy on the German model. The Great Mogul is in exile, and has taken lodgings at Kensington, with his only daughter, the Princess Rantrorina, who takes in needlework, and keeps a day school. *The princess is discovered hemming a set of shirts for the parson of the parish: they are to be marked with a large R. Enter to her the Great Mogul. A pause, during which they look at each other expressively. The princess changes color several times. The Mogul takes snuff in great agitation. Several grains are heard to fall on the stage. His heart is seen to beat through his upper benjamin.* — THE MOGUL (*with a mournful look at his left shoe*). 'My shoestring is broken.' — THE PRINCESS (*after an interval of melancholy reflection*). 'I know it.' — THE MOGUL. 'My second shoestring! The first broke when I lost my empire: the second has broken today. When will my poor heart break?' — THE PRINCESS. 'Shoestrings, hearts, and empires! Mysterious sympathy!'"

"Nonsense, sir," interrupted Mr. Glowry. "That is not at all like the voice I heard."

"But, sir," said Scythrop, "a keyhole may be so constructed as to act like an acoustic tube, and an acoustic tube, sir, will modify sound in a very remarkable manner. Consider the construction of the ear, and the nature and causes of sound. The external part of the ear is a cartilaginous funnel."

"It won't do, Scythrop. There is a girl concealed in

this tower, and find her I will. There are such things as sliding panels and secret closets." — He sounded round the room with his cane, but detected no hollowness. — "I have heard, sir," he continued, "that during my absence, two years ago, you had a dumb carpenter closeted with you day after day. I did not dream that you were laying contrivances for carrying on secret intrigues. Young men will have their way: I had my way when I was a young man: but, sir, when your cousin Marionetta —"

Scythrop now saw that the affair was growing serious. To have clapped his hand upon his father's mouth, to have entreated him to be silent, would, in the first place, not have made him so; and, in the second, would have shown a dread of being overheard by somebody. His only resource, therefore, was to try to drown Mr. Glowry's voice; and, having no other subject, he continued his description of the ear, raising his voice continually as Mr. Glowry raised his.

"When your cousin Marionetta," said Mr. Glowry, "whom you profess to love — whom you profess to love, sir —"

"The internal canal of the ear," said Scythrop, "is partly bony and partly cartilaginous. This internal canal is —"

"Is actually in the house, sir; and, when you are so shortly to be — as I expect —"

"Closed at the further end by the membrana tympani —"

"Joined together in holy matrimony —"

"Under which is carried a branch of the fifth pair of nerves —"

"I say, sir, when you are so shortly to be married to your cousin Marionetta —"

"The cavitas tympani —"

A loud noise was heard behind the bookcase, which,

to the astonishment of Mr. Glowry, opened in the middle, and the massy compartments, with all their weight of books, receding from each other in the manner of a theatrical scene, with a heavy rolling sound (which Mr. Glowry immediately recognized to be the same which had excited his curiosity,) disclosed an interior apartment, in the entrance of which stood the beautiful Stella, who, stepping forward, exclaimed, "Married! Is he going to be married? The profligate!"

"Really, madam," said Mr. Glowry, "I do not know what he is going to do, or what I am going to do, or what any one is going to do; for all this is incomprehensible."

"I can explain it all," said Scythrop, "in a most satisfactory manner, if you will but have the goodness to leave us alone."

"Pray, sir, to which act of the tragedy of the Great Mogul does this incident belong?"

"I entreat you, my dear sir, leave us alone."

Stella threw herself into a chair, and burst into a tempest of tears. Scythrop sat down by her, and took her hand. She snatched her hand away, and turned her back upon him. He rose, sat down on the other side, and took her other hand. She snatched it away, and turned from him again. Scythrop continued entreating Mr. Glowry to leave them alone; but the old gentleman was obstinate, and would not go.

"I suppose, after all," said Mr. Glowry maliciously, "it is only a phenomenon in acoustics, and this young lady is a reflection of sound from concave surfaces."

Some one tapped at the door: Mr. Glowry opened it, and Mr. Hilary entered. He had been seeking Mr. Glowry, and had traced him to Scythrop's tower. He stood a few moments in silent surprise, and then addressed himself to Mr. Glowry for an explanation.

"The explanation," said Mr. Glowry, "is very satisfactory. The Great Mogul has taken lodgings at Kensington, and the external part of the ear is a cartilaginous funnel."

"Mr. Glowry, that is no explanation."

"Mr. Hilary, it is all I know about the matter."

"Sir, this pleasantry is very unseasonable. I perceive that my niece is sported with in a most unjustifiable manner, and I shall see if she will be more successful in obtaining an intelligible answer." And he departed in search of Marionetta.

Scythrop was now in a hopeless predicament. Mr. Hilary made a hue and cry in the abbey, and summoned his wife and Marionetta to Scythrop's apartment. The ladies, not knowing what was the matter, hastened in great consternation. Mr. Toobad saw them sweeping along the corridor, and judging from their manner that the devil had manifested his wrath in some new shape, followed from pure curiosity.

Scythrop meanwhile vainly endeavored to get rid of Mr. Glowry and to pacify Stella. The latter attempted to escape from the tower, declaring she would leave the abbey immediately, and he should never see her or hear of her more. Scythrop held her hand and detained her by force, till Mr. Hilary reappeared with Mrs. Hilary and Marionetta. Marionetta, seeing Scythrop grasping the hand of a strange beauty, fainted away in the arms of her aunt. Scythrop flew to her assistance; and Stella with redoubled anger sprang towards the door, but was intercepted in her intended flight by being caught in the arms of Mr. Toobad, who exclaimed, "Celinda!"

"Papa!" said the young lady disconsolately.

"The devil is come among you," said Mr. Toobad, "how came my daughter here?"

"Your daughter!" exclaimed Mr. Glowry.

"Your daughter!" exclaimed Scythrop, and Mr. and Mrs. Hilary.

"Yes," said Mr. Toobad, "my daughter Celinda."

Marionetta opened her eyes and fixed them on Celinda; Celinda in return fixed hers on Marionetta. They were at remote points of the apartment. Scythrop was equidistant from both of them, central and motionless, like Mahomet's coffin.

"Mr. Glowry," said Mr. Toobad, "can you tell by what means my daughter came here?"

"I know no more," said Mr. Glowry, "than the Great Mogul."

"Mr. Scythrop," said Mr. Toobad, "how came my daughter here?"

"I did not know, sir, that the lady was your daughter."

"But how came she here?"

"By spontaneous locomotion," said Scythrop, sullenly.

"Celinda," said Mr. Toobad, "what does all this mean?"

"I really do not know, sir."

"This is most unaccountable. When I told you in London that I had chosen a husband for you, you thought proper to run away from him; and now, to all appearance, you have run away to him."

"How, sir! was that your choice?"

"Precisely; and if he is yours too we shall be both of a mind, for the first time in our lives."

"He is not my choice, sir. This lady has a prior claim: I renounce him."

"And I renounce him," said Marionetta. Scythrop knew not what to do. He could not attempt to conciliate the one without irreparably offending the other; and he was so fond of both, that the idea of depriving himself forever of the society of either was intolerable to him: he therefore retreated into his stronghold, mystery; maintained an impenetrable silence; and contented himself with stealing occasionally a deprecating glance at each of the objects of his idolatry. Mr. Toobad and Mr. Hilary, in the meantime, were each insisting on an explanation from Mr. Glowry, who they thought had been playing a double game on this occasion. Mr. Glowry was vainly endeavoring to persuade them of his innocence in the whole transaction. Mrs. Hilary was endeavoring to mediate between her husband and brother. The Honorable Mr. Listless, the Reverend Mr. Larynx, Mr. Flosky, Mr. Asterias, and Aquarius, were attracted by the tumult to the scene of action, and were appealed to severally and conjointly by the respective disputants. Multitudinous questions, and answers en masse, composed a charivari, to which the genius of Rossini alone could have given a suitable accompaniment, and which was only terminated by Mrs. Hilary and Mr. Toobad retreating with the captive damsels. The whole, party followed, with the exception of Scythrop, who threw himself into his armchair, crossed his left foot over his right knee, placed the hollow of his left hand on the interior ankle of his left leg, rested his right elbow on the elbow of the chair, placed the ball of his right thumb against his right temple, curved the forefinger along the upper part of his forehead, rested the point of the middle finger on the bridge of his nose, and the points of the two others on the lower part of the palm, fixed his eyes intently on the veins in the back of his left hand, and sat in this position like the immoveable Theseus, who, as is well known to many who have not been at college, and to some few who have, *sedet æternumque sedebit.* We hope the admirers of the minutiæ in poetry and romance will appreciate this accurate description of a pensive attitude.

Chapter XIV

*S*cythrop was still in this position when Raven entered to announce that dinner was on table.

"I cannot come," said Scythrop.

Raven sighed. "Something is the matter," said Raven: "but man is born to trouble."

"Leave me," said Scythrop: "go, and croak elsewhere."

"Thus it is," said Raven. "Five-and-twenty years have I lived in Nightmare Abbey, and now all the reward of my affection is — Go, and croak elsewhere. I have danced you on my knee, and fed you with marrow."

"Good Raven," said Scythrop, "I entreat you to leave me."

"Shall I bring your dinner here?" said Raven. "A boiled fowl and a glass of Madeira are prescribed by the faculty in cases of low spirits. But you had better join the party: it is very much reduced already."

"Reduced! how?"

"The Honorable Mr. Listless is gone. He declared that, what with family quarrels in the morning, and ghosts at night, he could get neither sleep nor peace; and that the agitation was too much for his nerves:

though Mr. Glowry assured him that the ghost was only poor Crow walking in his sleep, and that the shroud and bloody turban were a sheet and a red nightcap."

"Well, sir?"

"The Reverend Mr. Larynx has been called off on duty, to marry or bury (I don't know which) some unfortunate person or persons, at Claydyke: but man is born to trouble!"

"Is that all?"

"No. Mr. Toobad is gone too, and a strange lady with him."

"Gone!"

"Gone. And Mr. and Mrs. Hilary, and Miss O'Carroll: they are all gone. There is nobody left but Mr. Asterias and his son, and they are going tonight."

"Then I have lost them both."

"Won't you come to dinner?"

"No."

"Shall I bring your dinner here?"

"Yes."

"What will you have?"

"A pint of port and a pistol."

"A pistol!"

"And a pint of port. I will make my exit like Werter. Go. Stay. Did Miss O'Carroll say any thing?"

"No."

"Did Miss Toobad say any thing?"

"The strange lady? No."

"Did either of them cry?"

"No."

"What did they do?"

"Nothing."

"What did Mr. Toobad say?"

"He said, fifty times over, the devil was come among us."

"And they are gone?"

"Yes; and the dinner is getting cold. There is a time for everything under the sun. You may as well dine first, and be miserable afterwards."

"True, Raven. There is something in that. I will take your advice: therefore, bring me —"

"The port and the pistol?"

"No; the boiled fowl and Madeira."

Scythrop had dined, and was sipping his Madeira alone, immersed in melancholy musing, when Mr. Glowry entered, followed by Raven, who, having placed an additional glass and set a chair for Mr. Glowry, withdrew. Mr. Glowry sat down opposite Scythrop. After a pause, during which each filled and drank in silence, Mr. Glowry said, "So, sir, you have played your cards well. I proposed Miss Toobad to you: you refused her. Mr. Toobad proposed you to her: she refused you. You fell in love with Marionetta, and were going to poison yourself, because, from pure fatherly regard to your temporal interests, I withheld my consent. When, at length, I offered you my consent, you told me I was too precipitate. And, after all, I find you and Miss Toobad living together in the same tower, and behaving in every respect like two plighted lovers. Now, sir, if there be any rational solution of all this absurdity, I shall be very much obliged to you for a small glimmering of information."

"The solution, sir, is of little moment; but I will leave it in writing for your satisfaction. The crisis of my fate is come: the world is a stage, and my direction is exit."

"Do not talk so, sir; — do not talk so, Scythrop. What would you have?"

"I would have my love."

"And pray, sir, who is your love?"

"Celinda — Marionetta — either — both."

"Both! That may do very well in a German tragedy;

and the Great Mogul might have found it very feasible in his lodgings at Kensington; but it will not do in Lincolnshire. Will you have Miss Toobad?"

"Yes."

"And renounce Marionetta?"

"No."

"But you must renounce one."

"I cannot."

"And you cannot have both. What is to be done?"

"I must shoot myself."

"Don't talk so, Scythrop. Be rational, my dear Scythrop. Consider, and make a cool, calm choice, and I will exert myself in your behalf."

"Why should I choose, sir? Both have renounced *me*: I have no hope of either."

"Tell me which you will have, and I will plead your cause irresistibly."

"Well, sir, — I will have — no, sir, I cannot renounce either. I cannot choose either. I am doomed to be the victim of eternal disappointments; and I have no resource but a pistol."

"Scythrop — Scythrop; — if one of them should come to you — what then?"

"That, sir, might alter the case: but that cannot be."

"It can be, Scythrop; it will be: I promise you it will be. Have but a little patience — but a week's patience; and it shall be.

"A week, sir, is an age: but, to oblige you, as a last act of filial duty, I will live another week. It is now Thursday evening, twenty-five minutes past seven. At this hour and minute, on Thursday next, love and fate shall smile on me, or I will drink my last pint of port in this world."

Mr. Glowry ordered his traveling chariot, and departed from the abbey.

Chapter XV

The day after Mr. Glowry's departure was one of incessant rain, and Scythrop repented of the promise he had given. The next day was one of bright sunshine: he sat on the terrace, read a tragedy of Sophocles, and was not sorry, when Raven announced dinner, to find himself alive. On the third evening, the wind blew, and the rain beat, and the owl flapped against his windows; and he put a new flint in his pistol. On the fourth day, the sun shone again; and he locked the pistol up in a drawer, where he left it undisturbed, till the morning of the eventful Thursday, when he ascended the turret with a telescope, and spied anxiously along the road that crossed the fens from Claydyke: but nothing appeared on it. He watched in this manner from ten A.M. till Raven summoned him to dinner at five; when he stationed Crow at the telescope, and descended to his own funeral-feast. He left open the communications between the tower and turret, and called aloud at intervals to Crow, — "Crow, Crow, is any thing coming?" Crow answered, "The wind blows, and the windmills turn, but I see nothing coming;" and, at every answer, Scythrop found the necessity of raising his

spirits with a bumper. After dinner, he gave Raven his
watch to set by the abbey clock. Raven brought it,
Scythrop placed it on the table, and Raven departed.
Scythrop called again to Crow; and Crow, who had
fallen asleep, answered mechanically, "I see nothing
coming." Scythrop laid his pistol between his watch
and his bottle. The hour-hand passed the VII. — the
minute-hand moved on; — it was within three minutes
of the appointed time. Scythrop called again to Crow:
Crow answered as before. Scythrop rang the bell: Raven
appeared.

"Raven," said Scythrop, "the clock is too fast."

"No, indeed," said Raven, who knew nothing of
Scythrop's intentions; "if any thing, it is too slow."

"Villain!" said Scythrop, pointing the pistol at him;
"it is too fast."

"Yes — yes — too fast, I meant," said Raven, in
manifest fear.

"How much too fast?" said Scythrop.

"As much as you please," said Raven.

"How much, I say?" said Scythrop, pointing the
pistol again.

"An hour, a full hour, sir," said the terrified butler.

"Put back my watch," said Scythrop.

Raven, with trembling hand, was putting back the
watch, when the rattle of wheels was heard in the court;
and Scythrop, springing down the stairs by three steps
together, was at the door in sufficient time to have
handed either of the young ladies from the carriage, if
she had happened to be in it; but Mr. Glowry was
alone.

"I rejoice to see you," said Mr. Glowry; "I was fearful
of being too late, for I waited till the last moment in
the hope of accomplishing my promise; but all my
endeavors have been vain, as these letters will show."

Scythrop impatiently broke the seals. The contents
were these:

Almost a stranger in England, I fled from parental tyranny, and the dread of an arbitrary marriage, to the protection of a stranger and a philosopher, whom I expected to find something better than, or at least something different from, the rest of his worthless species. Could I, after what has occurred, have expected nothing more from you than the commonplace impertinence of sending your father to treat with me, and with mine, for me? I should be a little moved in your favor, if I could believe you capable of carrying into effect the resolutions which your father says you have taken, in the event of my proving inflexible; though I doubt not you will execute them, as far as relates to the pint of wine, twice over, at least. I wish you much happiness with Miss O'Carroll. I shall always cherish a grateful recollection of Nightmare Abbey, for having been the means of introducing me to a true transcendentalist; and, though he is a little older than myself, which is all one in Germany, I shall very soon have the pleasure of subscribing myself

Celinda Flosky

I hope, my dear cousin, that you will not be angry with me, but that you will always think of me as a sincere friend, who will always feel interested in your welfare; I am sure you love Miss Toobad much better than me, and I wish you much happiness with her. Mr. Listless assures me that people do not kill themselves for love nowadays, though it is still the fashion to talk about it. I shall, in a very short time, change my name and situation, and shall always be happy to see you in Berkeley Square, when, to the unalterable designation of your affectionate cousin, I shall subjoin the signature of

MARIONETTA LISTLESS

Scythrop tore both the letters to atoms, and railed in good set terms against the fickleness of women.

"Calm yourself, my dear Scythrop," said Mr. Glowry; "there are yet maidens in England."

"Very true, sir," said Scythrop.

"And the next time," said Mr. Glowry, "have but one string to your bow."

"Very good advice, sir," said Scythrop.

"And, besides," said Mr. Glowry, "the fatal time is past, for it is now almost eight."

"Then that villain, Raven," said Scythrop, "deceived me when he said that the clock was too fast; but, as you observe very justly, the time has gone by, and I have just reflected that these repeated crosses in love qualify me to take a very advanced degree in misanthropy; and there is, therefore, good hope that I may make a figure in the world. But I shall ring for the rascal Raven, and admonish him."

Raven appeared. Scythrop looked at him very fiercely two or three minutes; and Raven, still remembering the pistol, stood quaking in mute apprehension, till Scythrop, pointing significantly towards the dining room, said, "Bring some Madeira."

Printed in the United Kingdom
by Lightning Source UK
102568UKS00002B/201